Countess di Brazzà

A guide to old and new lace in Italy

Countess di Brazzà

A guide to old and new lace in Italy

ISBN/EAN: 9783742839695

Manufactured in Europe, USA, Canada, Australia, Japa

Cover: Foto ©Andreas Hilbeck / pixelio.de

Manufactured and distributed by brebook publishing software
(www.brebook.com)

Countess di Brazzà

A guide to old and new lace in Italy

A GUIDE TO

Old and New Lace in Italy

Exhibited at Chicago in 1893.

DEDICATED TO

HER MAJESTY QUEEN MARGHERITA,

BY

W. B. CONKEY COMPANY,
341-351 DEARBORN STREET, CHICAGO,
1893.

HER MAJESTY QUEEN MARGHERITA.

TO HER MAJESTY

Margherita of Savoja,

QUEEN OF ITALY.

YOUR MAJESTY:

Many words were in my heart and floated uncrystallized across my mind, with which to dedicate the work of our Lace Committee and this little Guide Book to Your Majesty, when my eyes rested upon the following lines by Aurelio Passerotti, at the beginning of his Pattern Book for noble lace makers, the only known copy of which belongs to Count Nerio Malvezzi of Bologna. Here are mirrored all my thoughts, gracefully clothed in that old time phraseology which is as intricately and delicately wrought as the subtile fabric to whose treasury it serves as a key, and whose gracious mistress it so respectfully lauds.

I therefore pray Your Majesty to accept this tribute of another time to another Royal Margherita, who, in that portion of the land over which she reigned, loved to protect and to encourage the arts of peace, as does Your Majesty throughout United Italy.

Cora Slocomb di Brazzà.

...PREFACE...

❖

THIS is not only a guide book descriptive of the unique collection of antique laces from all parts of the world exhibited in the Italian section of the Woman's Building, at the World's Columbian Exposition, held in Chicago during the summer of 1893, and kindly lent by Our Most Gracious Queen Margherita and the ladies of Italy, whose names follow on the list of Directresses and Patronesses.

It opens with a description of every kind of lace-like fabric, and forms a *complete and succinct history of lace from its origin to the present day ;* it contains a biographical sketch of those artists who entrusted to us their finest works, all of which are for sale that there might be a worthy framing to the rarer laces.

It also has appended a list of the books exhibited, which form a small and interesting library, and complete collection of antique designs for lace-makers and embroiderers, compiled by the editor, and placed for reference and study at the disposal of those visitors whom they may interest.

Finally and above all, it contains descriptive notices of all the Lace Schools and Lace Manufactories in Italy, founded or directed by women, with which the committee has been able to communicate in the short time between its organization and the shipping of the exhibit to Chicago. These notices are illustrated by photographs and very complete albums of samples, as well as by large quantities of the laces Italian women produce, which are for sale with immediate delivery. For any information or purchases of books or laces, visitors are begged to address themselves to the lady attendant, remembering that every piece of lace sold, however insignificant it may seem, means at least one hearty meal for some poor and industrious woman, some fatherless, dumb or crippled child in Italy.

PART I.

INTRODUCTION.

A Descriptive Enumeration of the most Celebrated Laces of the Past.

For a clear understanding of any chapter of the second part or history of lace making, without reading the one preceding it, it is necessary thoroughly to comprehend and to impress upon the mind the following terms and their meanings, remembering that the older and kindred arts from which lace-making sprang, are very nearly allied to it, and often produce such similar effects that it is impossible for the uninitiated to distinguish between them.

Patronesses Residing in Foreign Countries.

	Lire.
Signora A. Ravagli for the Italian Colony in Cincinnati, United States of America	295 25
The Consul for the Italian Colony in Chicago, United States of America	129 60
Countess di Cesnola, New York, United States of America	125 00
Baroness Fava, Legation at Washington, United States of America.	100 00
Signora Bruni Grimaldi, Denver, United States of America	100 00
Countess Galli nata Roberts, Paris, France	103 50
Marchesa Mariad Adda Salvaterra nata Hooker, Paris, France	100 00
Total	953 35
Contributions received from the Royal Ministry of Commerce and Agriculture	1,000

RECAPITULATION.

I	Venetia	4,708
II	Roman Provinces	2,020
III	Tuscany	1,989
IV	Sicily	1,883
V	Lombardy	1,510
VI	Romagna	1,187
VII	Liguria	1,100
VIII	Naples	900
IX	Piedmont	450
X	Emilia	260
XI	Umbria	200
XII	Abruzzi	100
XIII	Marche	100
XIV	Sardegna	100
	Patronesses residing in foreign countries	953 35
	Contribution from the Royal Ministry of Agriculture and Commerce	1,000
	Total	18,460 35

Donation from the Countess di Brazza to assist in defraying the expenses of the Lace exhibit—all the proceeds of the author as royalty on the sale of this book.

I.—PASSAMANO OR PASSAMENTERIE.
(Gimp, and Knotted Fringes or Trimmings.)
Their Manufacture.

These trimmings or adornments are now made by means of a long, narrow, bolster-shaped cushion screwed to a table; on this cushion the fringed-out stuff or a foundation cord is held in place by large headed pins around which are knotted, in various patterns, the threads that are to form the fringe or edging; in the coarser work, the fingers alone suffice to tie the knots but for finer effects, the use of the crochet needle is necessary. To prepare a textile for its conversion into an ornamental knotted border, the woof threads are drawn out, leaving a portion of the warp of the width required for the fringe, the selvedge is cut away and the threads are knotted as desired. Extra tassels are sometimes added for a finish.

Different Varieties.

Macrame is a modification of the ordinary passamenterie. Different kinds of macrame are known as:

Punto a Groppo, knotted point.

Punto Moresco, or Moorish point.

Punto a Groppo Incordonato, or corded, knotted point. The above are all terms used by the Venetians for this class of work.

II.—RETE (net), AND MAGLIA (knitting).
Manufacture of Knitting.

For the single stitches of both the Italians have one generic term, viz., "*Maglia*" knitting. *Punto a Maglia* is made with two long, blunt needles of wood, steel or bone held one in each hand; over them a thread is knotted in and out continuously until a flexible, elastic material is formed which is more or less ornate according to the object for which it is destined and the fancy of the knitter.

Manufacture of Net.

Rete (*net*) is made by means of a wooden, brass or bone needle, bifurcated at either end, around which the thread or cord is wound; a little stick is also used the width of which must be half the depth of the stitches or meshes required. The end of the netting cord or thread is knotted in a loop to a solid peg; holding the stick in the left hand, the needle charged with the cord is passed around the stick, through the loop, and in and out again through the first twist made which is held in place by the stick and thus forms a knot. The stick is then removed and another mesh is begun.

Different Varieties.

Frivolite (*tatting*). For this the little stick is replaced by the fingers of the left hand and more complicated knots of different varieties are made.

Modano, a very ancient net lace that is made without any embroidery is quite artistic in effect. The meshes of Modano may be large or small, round, square or shell-shaped, according to the size and form of the stick which is held in the left hand and the number of meshes taken or skipped in knotting into the row above. This netting can be varied indefinitely; it is often very pretty and to the untrained eye, it greatly resembles some of the varieties of pillow lace.

Manufacture of Laces:

Merletto a Maglia or *Maglietta* (*laces or net lace*).

Merletto a Maglia Quadrata (*square net lace*).

Merletto a Retine Ricamate (*embroidered net lace.*)

These are all terms used for the embroidered nets that were so much the fashion in the middle ages.

After making meshes of the size and number desired to compose the net foundation, this is sown firmly to a metal frame, wound with tape, which keeps it perfectly stretched, for on this greatly depends the beauty of the finished work; the design is then embroidered with a needle and thread upon the net in varied stitches, the principal ones used being darning, wheel and button-hole.

III.—PUNTO TIRATO OR PUNTO DISFATTO (drawn work) PUNTO TAGLIATO (cut work).

These titles comprise all the earliest attempts to produce needle lace; the most elaborate varieties might really be treated as point laces if judged simply by their appearances; these laces are worked in linen or lawn.

Manufacture of Burato.

Burato is an embroidery wrought with the needle, in which drawn work, outlining and cross-stitch are combined. It is finely spun though coarsely woven fabrics, and was used on underwear and household linen.

Punto in Stuora (*sheeting or curtain stitch*), also called Trapunto. This is made with silk or thread, forming what people commonly call *Sicilian embroidery or lace*; the ground of this lace instead of being drawn and embroidered in the textile, is often made with bobbins, the threads of which form a kind of very coarse, twisted gauze, or fine net, on which the designs are afterward embroidered.

Manufacture of Punto Tagliato (*cut work*). The design for this work was first traced on a piece of linen which was then drawn very smoothly over a leaf of parchment attached to a hair cushion, called a "*balon*," and firmly basted down. This completed, a coarse thread was sewed along the traced outline, and a *Punto a Festone*, or button-hole stitch, was worked over this around the entire design; then, very carefully cutting away the intervening material that none of the threads composing the stitching might be frayed, double parallel threads were drawn from angle to angle of the empty spaces; these threads were often elaborately intercrossed and button-holed to enriching the design, or they were caught around pins at the border, forming an edging of purled loops called *cechetti* and *smerli*.

Different Varieties.

Punto Calabrese (*Calabrian work*) very closely resembles the last but it is adorned with high reliefs.

IV.—PUNTO A RETICELLA RADIXELLI (NET POINTS).

Manufacture of Reticella.

This stitch consists in a combination of drawn and cut work, no design was traced, but the threads of the linen were counted and drawn out in such manner as to form alternate squares in which the warp alone was then cut away, and the remaining threads were used as a foundation which was button-holed over the open spaces between being filled as in *Punto Tagliato*—with fancy stitches.

Punto Surana was a kind of *Recticella* with oriental designs.

Punto Greco and *Punto di Zante*, were names given to the same kind of work coming from Greece and the Archipelago.

Punto Reale, or *Royal point* was the contrary of *Reticella* although executed in the same manner, for in it the linen ground was left and the design was made by cutting out open spaces and then filling them in with fancy stitches.

Punto di Cartella or *Cardella* (*card work*) was a lace having a similar effect to that of *Reticella*, but, instead of having the ground made by drawn work, the button-holing was done entirely on a foundation made by sewing coarse shreds of parchment on a most carefully drawn design and then covering them with button-hole stitch.

The most celebrated edgings in Reticella were known under the following names:

Punti d'Arcato (*Arched points*). When the loops or *smerli* of the edge became deep and more ornate they received this distinctive appellation.

Punti Fiamenghi (*Flemish points*), these were rectangular and therefore rather broad and shallow, they were often alternated in two sizes, placed close together but always retained the same form.

Punti Spagnuoli (*Spanish points*), were like the preceding, save that they were all of the same size and much longer, narrower and more pointed, and surrounded by elaborate small *smerli*.

Punti Gaetani were a combination of Spanish and Flemish

points held together by *smerli* at one third or half their depth; they were filled in with the usual stitches producing a varied effect which resembled a double row of *smerlatura* or *turretting*. There were many other fancy stitches, generally known in Italy at the beginning of the sixteenth century, which continued in use after the introduction of the real *points*, or needle laces, produced exclusively with a needle and thread, the textile foundation no longer being found necessary in that more elaborate and perfected lace. Some of these stitches were known as:

Punto Damaschino, or *Damascus point.*

Punto a Filo or *Punto a Festone* a variety of *button hole stitch.*

Punto Rilevato, *raised stitch,* or *stitch in relief.*

Punto Sopra Punto, *loop stitch in relief.*

Punto Ingarseato, *gauze stitch* (used as a filling in stitch).

Punto Ciprioto, Cyprus stitch, with an effect resembling the open work ground in Greek and Turkish embroidery.

Punto Pugliese, which resembled Russian and Roumania embroidery, etc. In fact wherever lace was made there were also local terms as is the case in every other industry.

V.—POINT LACES.

Manufacture of Point Lace.

Point laces are made entirely with the needle and are as susceptible to the surrounding influences and climate, people and national characteristics as are the architecture, sculpture and paintings of different countries. This delicate art is indeed so sensitive to change that, strange as it may seem, the same patterns wrought by lace-makers of neighboring towns and villages, produce entirely different effects. There are, however, unalterable general rules which are followed everywhere, namely, that the design must first be very carefully drawn upon a piece of parchment which has been so tinted as to form a dark back-ground, and a large thread (or several fine threads twisted together) must be sewn with great exactness around the edges of all the flowers, scrolls and other figures of the design as a foundation, using as few stitches in this as possible, because these stitches are after-

ward cut away; all the figures of the design are then filled in between the outlining threads with close and varied stitches; the
ground is then made with net-work (tulle stitch) like *Burano
point*, or with purled guipure, like Venetian point; lastly the
foundation threads which follow the edges of the design are button-holed over, more or less elaborately, to form the reliefs.   The
lace is detached carefully from the parchment foundation by cutting the fastening threads and the different pieces composing the
desired length are sewed together, the finishing touches being
added by an especially skilled worker.   In the making of point
lace the needle-women are usually divided into six different sec-
tions, to each of which a different portion of the work is allotted,
such as grounding, tulling, etc., thus affording not only greater
rapidity but more skilled execution.

Punto di Venezia, or *Venetian point*, also called *parchment lace*.
This is a comprehensive term under which the following varieties of needle laces with open grounds are known; the *Punto di
Venezia*, properly so-called, differs from the *Punto in Aria* only in
having the scrolls farther apart, more insignificant in design, and
surrounded by button-hole stitch.

Varieties of Venetian Point.

Punto in Aria (lace worked in **air**).   In this lace the flowers,
scrolls and designs of animals were wrought in very fine thread
in varied open work composed of very small stitches; the threads
forming the foundation were then button-holed over before the
filling in of the design, and the whole was held in place where
the design did not connect the parts with button-holed purled
loops or guipure bars.

Punto ad Avorio (*ivory point*) was a variety of the above with
designs copied from the beautiful flowered scrolls of the *intarcia*
(inlaid) work of the sixteenth century; being made with very
close stitches and low reliefs which produced a solid effect.   It
looked as though carved in ivory and justified this distinctive
appellation.

Punto dei Nobili, or *cardinal lace*, was especially manufactured for marriages, births and grand family or civic festivals.

Its designs pictured warriors on foot, or on horseback, hunts, castles, towns, animals, cardinal's hats and princely crowns, gods, goddesses and mermaids—in fact nearly every kind of object, real or imaginary; in case of a treaty or a marriage, the arms of the contracting parties were liberally introduced into the design of the lace destined to be used on the occasion.

Punto tagliato a Fogliame (*flowered lace*). This is a lace composed of scrolls and flowers that seem literally *carved* in flax. It is the richest point lace ever invented, and formerly it was made in silk, gold or silver as well as thread. Using the *Punto in Aria* as a foundation to produce this lace, stitches are made upon stitches, and row is super-added upon row of button-holing. The flowers were formerly packed with horse hair instead of with thread, that they might stand out in fuller, richer reliefs, detaching themselves more perfectly from the ground-work, or foundation. All around the edges of these wonderful blossoms and scrolls, and upon the sides and pinnacles of every relief were then made, with infinite patience, thousands upon thousands of microscopic loops, sometimes five or six rows deep, resembling more the delicate flowers and fairy landscapes seen in hoar frost than the work of even the daintiest human fingers. Modifications of this celebrated lace, sung by poets, described by historians, and a source of commercial rivalry between powerful potentates, were known as:

Punto di Spagna; point made in Spain.

Grand Point de France, also called *Point Colbert,* from the minister of Louis XIV, who introduced it into his country from Venice.

Punto di Neve (*snow point*), which was very beautiful with its ground of starred threads that resemble flakes of snow.

Punto di Rosa (*rose point*). The bars of this lace were placed close together, forming a regular, sexagonal network-ground, with innumerable raised flowers and tiny scrolls composing the design.

Punto a Fogliame (*leaf point*), with graceful blooms and tendrils predominating in the design, and many loops upon their edges, like the denticulated margins of leaves and flowers.

Punto a Giole (*jewelled point*), is frequently mentioned by old writers, although no example of it is left for the instruction of the industrial artists of to-day. It was into this lace that pearls and other gems, and even the colored Venetian beads that so closely resemble gems, were wrought by skilled artists, producing a most gorgeous effect; this lace was also varied by using silk, gold or silver instead of linen thread as a foundation or to form the reliefs.

BURANO POINT AND THE LACES TO WHICH IT GAVE ORIGIN.

Punto di Burano is so called from the place of its manufacture, Burano, an island in the lagoon east of Venice. This flowered point lace with a gauze ground was very highly prized, and the following celebrated laces were all copied from it.

Argentella; a fine needle-point lace resembling the *Burano point*, but with a curious kind of spider-web ground introduced. Mrs. Bury Paliser says it was invented in Genoa, but we believe that it is the Italian term for early Argentan lace, for there are no proofs of needle lace ever having flourished in Genoa or its environs.

POINT D'ALENCON, AND POINT D'ARGENTAN.

The manufacture of these laces was introduced into France under Louis XIV, through the importation, and at great expense, of Italian lace makers, to teach their art to the lace makers of France who, of course, modified it. These laces copied from the antique designs are now produced in as great perfection in the co-operative lace schools of Burano as they were a hundred years ago, the time of their greatest glory, in France.

Point d'Alencon, has the same square mesh ground as *Burano point*, but it is not quite as fine as that of the early Buranese specimens, the outlines of the reliefs, serving as foundation, were frequently formed of horse hair, covered by the usual button-hole stitch and purled.

Point d'Argentan. The ground meshes of this lace are larger than those of the *Point d'Alencon* and their sexagonal form is perfect, and frequently composed entirely of microscopic button-holing which increases immensely the value of the lace in it. The flower designs have a much closer filling and the open work spaces are larger and more varied in their stitches than those of *Point d'Alençon.*

Vieux Point de Bruxelles (*old Brussels point*) exactly resembles the earliest *Burano point,* the distinction between them consisting in its ground stitch being slightly rounder than that of *Burano point.*

Mixed Points.

Point de Bruxelles (*modern Brussels lace*) is composed of flowers, scrolls and ribbons of needle point sewed upon a fine, machine-made tulle which is cut out beneath the flower, after which the whole is so perfectly darned together that the lace appears as if made in one piece.

Point Plat, in *Brussels lace* is so called when the flowers and scrolls transferred to the net are, as in *Honiton Lace,* made entirely with bobbins.

Duchess Lace, or *Point d'Application,* resembles the Brussels Point Plat, the only difference being that in the *Duchesse lace* the tulle foundation is not cut away.

The tulle or meshes in *old Brussels bobbin lace* are hexagonal in form; four of the sides of the mesh are composed of two threads twisted together twice, and two of the sides are composed of four threads plaited together four times.

Honiton, or *English Point,* resembles *Duchesse lace* when made with a tulle ground, as, if an all-over design of flowers be desired, the workwomen execute each branch of blossoms separately and these are afterward united by purled bars.

English Needle Lace has never been manufactured in large quantities but was always copied from Italian, French or Belgian lace; it therefore has no distinctive terminology.

In the last twenty years a lace composed of narrow, machine or hand-made braid and point lace stitches, has become fashionable in England; as fancy work some of the designs are very good and the stitches are pleasantly varied. This lace is really a revival of *Punto di Ragusa,* but it is much less artistic, having a meagre appearance; it is generally called *Point* without any other definition.   Sometimes it is called *braided lace;* in Italy it is known as *Guipure a Spighetta Inglese,* or *English Braided Guipure.*

Venetian Guipure was a mixed point lace. The scroll work and flowers in it were outlined in pillow lace, then the designs were filled in and reliefs were made with the needle, the ground being composed of purled bars, this lace was somtimes made in silk with pleasing effect.

Turkish Point is a fine needle lace made on the edge of oriental stuffs, it is artistic and very original. It is composed entirely of one stitch, that of the *Punto in Aria* without any button-holing, or ground, or connecting loops sometimes it is made in imitation of flowers and fruits in their natural colors, or all of white silk with gold and silver threads introduced. At others it forms a narrow edging composed of simple, geometric designs.

Irish Point is made on fine batiste by stitching a coarse thread all around the design and then cutting out the groundwork and filling in the open spaces, sometimes with connecting loops and knots, and at other times with *Punto in Aria.*

Irish Guipure is made with a crochet needle and fine linen thread; its designs are copied from the best old patterns, and it is frequently very artistic.

Broiderie des Indes.   When Indian muslin scarfs with their exquisite open work lace stitches were introduced into Europe, all laces made on a muslin ground received this name, even though they had been produced prior to the origin of this fashion, some specimens of this embroidery made in the seventeenth and eighteenth centuries looks exactly like Venetian or Burano Point lace.

VI.—MERELTTO A FUSELLI (Bobbin Lace).

Merletto a Tombola, *Pillow Lace,* or *Merletto a Piombini.* This lace derives its name from the word *"Piombare"* which signifies to hang vertically, as a plummet. It can be made of cotton, flax, fibre, gold or silver thread.   In its fabrication a quantity of threads are interwoven in various stitches; the meshes and openings or agiorni are made by introducing pins into the design and twisting threads about them in divers ways, as in *Point Lace*, the effects produced are varied, but the system employed is always the same, as follows: Around a roller-shaped cushion, which is stuffed with chopped hay, sawdust or wool, and is covered with some dark woolen stuff, is carefully stretched the design which has first been drawn upon stiff paper and then pricked out along the outline of the drawing. The cushion is then placed upon a little rest, shaped to fit it on the one side and to fit the knees on the other, or it is placed upon a stand in front of the work-woman or grasped between the knees. From right to left the thread is wound rapidly upon the bobbins and tied at the top in a loop that permits it to gradually slip off the bobbin when gently pulled, as occurs continuously in working. The bobbins themselves are tiny clyinders of wood with a knot at the top. All the threads are then attached to hat pins that have been stuck firmly in the cushion to give a good purchase hold, and the lace maker is ready to go to work. She begins by interlacing the bob-bins, which are used in pairs, and placing small pins in all the per-forations—u—crossing the bobbins after the insertion of each pin. The bobbins not in use are kept from becoming entangled by large hat pins that hold them back on either side of the design. Some-times a coarse thread follows the entire outline to make the pattern more marked. The throwing back of certain bobbins, so as leave them out in the middle of a flower or scroll, and then take them back into the design after a little produces the raised work that is called *Punto riportato sopra*. As the manufacture of the lace pro-ceeds (being worked from left to right and right to left alter-nately) the furthermost pins are removed, as required, to place in the holes last reached, thus detaching the lace from the cushion and allowing it to be cut off at any length desired. A coarse thread is sometimes run around the design with a needle, after it is finished and entirely removed from the cushion, but can not equal in effect that worked in as the lace proceeds.

GUIPURES.

Guipure is a very old verb, meaning "to roll a thread around a card." In the early part of the sixteenth century lace always contained a *guip*, which formed the pattern, and the term has been preserved. Although the card, or parchment, has long fallen into disuse, and this word, in modern parlance, is applied to any lace with geometric designs, conventionalized flowers, or arabesques, held together by a grounding of purled loops or bars, in contradistinction to other laces that are made with an all-over net ground. As bobbin laces are easily and rapidly executed—they are made all over the civilized world—with perpetual re-duplication, and yet with almost endless variety in design. Some of the most celebrated among the guipures are:

Maltese Point, or *Punto di Malta* from which the famous *Genoese guipure* was copied; its designs were always highly ornamental and its edge was composed of very deep indentations, much resmbling the Moorish decorations of the Alhambra. It will be remembered that flowers and animals were never pictured in early Arabian work; therefore, they are absent from all laces inspired by the designs of Mahometan artists.

Guipure di Genoa is, as has been indicated, the counterpart of *Punto di Malta.*

Punto di Genoa, also sometimes called *Guipure di Milano,* so greatly resembles the Milanese and Neapolitan that it is easily confused with them. The difference which renders it recognizable consists in the scroll work of the design, which, in the Genoese, as in the Spanish flat guipure, is composed of a broader, more varied ribbon than in the Milanese and Neapolitan laces. A very fine quality of this lace is called *Fugio* (meaning "I fly"), a name given as much on account of its soft airiness as on account of the running scrolls of which it is entirely composed. In all these laces a crochet needle is used to join the bars together to the design. In order to do this one thread is drawn with it through a pin-hole in the lace, thus forming a loop, and then the knot is closed by passing the free bobbin of the pair through this loop and simply closing the loop so as to insure added solidity in knotting the bobbins.

Guipure Flamengo or *Flemish Guipure,* can not be distinguished, save by experts, from *Spanish flat lace,* much of this having been made in Flanders, to furnish the Spanish market. Varieties of this lace were made all over Europe and were introduced into the colonies of Italy, Spain and Portugal by the nuns.

Russian lace and Hungarian lace are varieties of the Flemish guipure, which are produced by following the same principles in their manufacture, although the designs are characteristic of the countries in which they are made.

Punto di Ragusa was made like the *Genoese and Milanese laces*, save that its ribbon of bobbin lace was edged on one or both sides with a thick cord sometimes increased in size—as in the *Venetian Point*—by winding thread around horse-hair, or by button-holing over the edge of the braid after basting a cord upon it. *Venetian* and *Ragusa guipures* are often spoken of as identical, but they are quite different in effect and execution, the *Punto di Ragusa* having a decidedly Byzantine character.

Merletto Greco, or *Greek Guipure*, has also one or two cords following the curves of the braid, but its effect is much less rich than that of the *Punto di Ragusa*.

Cartisane is one of the earliest and rarest of lace guipures; it was made of a coarse torchon lace composed by making four twists and then four plats alternately with the bobbin. Through these meshes were wrought simple and artistic arabesque designs with two or more strips of thick paper or vellum, each wound with fine silk to resemble a ribbon and held in place by pins until the lace was completed. The edges of this primitive trimming were straight and unornamented. As this lace did not wash well, its manufacture was soon abandoned.

Punto di Rapallo, or *Liguria*, is formed by a ribbon or braid of close lace following the outline of the design, which is composed of loops, filled in from time to time, with fancy gauze stitches made by knotting in extra bobbins with a crochet needle, and forming quaint geometrical reliefs. The especial characteristic of this lace, is that the braid is constantly thrown over the piece just made, thus forming large loops in the scrolls. The parts of the entire design are held together by purled guipure "brides" or bars.

Punto a Vermicelli is a modification of the *Punto di Rapallo*, in which the braid is made very fine and narrow; the trimmings are extremely complicated, and there are no fancy stitches between.

Merletto Polichrome, *parti-colored lace*, was invented and perfected by the Jews and was made in silk of different colors representing fruits and flowers. This industry has been revived in Venice and carried to great perfection.

VII.—PILLOW LACES WITH NET AND MIXED GROUNDS.

The most celebrated of these laces are all known under the general name of *Flanders Point*, and many of them are as fine as the subtlest cobwebs.

Varieties.

Point d' Angleterre is a superb and especially fine variety of Brussels pillow lace, with mixed ground. It is characterized by a raised rib of plaited threads worked at the same time as the rest of the lace. This rib outlines all the veinings and other salient points of the design, rendering it beautifully artistic. *Point d' Angleterre* generally represents garlands and other floral designs, and sometimes birds, figures and architectural details are introduced. It owes its name to having been originally made to smuggle into England and to sell as English lace; and to it was given a type entirely different from the older Brussels pillow lace. It was widely known and most especially appreciated in France and Italy, always retaining, however, its distinctive appellation. The meshes of which its ground is composed are sexagonal, with four of the sides consisting of two threads twisted twice and two of the sides of four threads plaited four times.

Mechlin, or *Malines,* is so named from the Flemish town where it was originally manufactured. It has a very fine mesh as ground sexagonal in form, with four of its sides made by twisting two threads together twice, while four threads are plaited together three times to form the other two sides. The ground is generally strewn with tiny spots, flowers or leaves, surrounded by one coarse, or several fine threads; flowers or leaves, or both, alternated, form the pattern along the heading, the same form being regularly and closely repeated like a flower chain, and the edge

is more or less undulated according to the design of the border.
The old Mechlin laces were sometimes rendered more elaborate
by introducing vases, in memory of the Annunciation; flowered
hearts, or other emblems, with openwork centers, but even these
always retained the detached and self-repeating quality which
became the distinguishing characteristic of this lace after the
middle of the seventeenth century.

Old Flemish Point, properly so-called, was made with a very
close ground, resembling squarish cobwebs, with round pin-holes
between the parts to outline the design. It consists of running
patterns composed of conventionalized fruit and flowers frequently
interlaced with a ribbon design which contains open-work and
adds lightness to the whole effect. Its edge was straight, with
tiny purls.

Trolle Kant resembles the *old Flemish Point,* but its ground is
clearer, with rounder webs, and the designs are surrounded by a
coarse thread, or a number of threads, wound on one bobbin.
The pattern is always so composed as to combine with the edge
of the lace forming shallow undulations or varied scallops,
finished off like all Flemish laces—with purls.

Antique Brussels pillow lace. The designs of this lace
resemble those of *Trolle Kant,* but it has a net or tulle ground
composed of a round or hexagonal mesh, or a combination of
both.

Antwerp lace was especially celebrated for trimming caps.
All the laces made in Brussels were imitated in Antwerp, but
this city also had an especial lace of its own, called *Potten Kant,*
in which the design—a vase—was worked like antique Brussels
lace, except that the net of which the ground was formed consisted of triangles with hexagonal meshes or openings.

English trolly lace was formerly made in Buckinghamshire,
and was copied from *Potten Kant,* just as the *baby lace,* made in
Bedford, Buckingham and Northampton, was a modification of
the *Lille lace,* and was sometimes called *English Point de Lille.*

Binche is a most exquisite cobwebby pillow lace from the
Province of Hainault, in Flanders. It contains designs of flowers,
fruits and figures wrought of the finest, most fairylike thread,

connected by tiny rounds or discs, of close weaving, with mazes of intertwined threads holding the whole together, as though the designer had tried to picture a Dutch flower garden in a snow storm. This beautiful lace has a straight edge, and the finer qualities, which are no longer made, have become priceless.

Closter Spitze, or *Convent lace.* The manufacture of this lace was originally confined, as the name indicates, to convents, especially to those in the north of Europe. The present center of its production is, at Bohemia. The treatment of the design and the grounding are identical with those of *Binche Point;* but, unlike this lace, it is coarse, though sheer and effective. Modified by the vicinity of *Milanese Point, Closter Spitze* was also made in southern Tyrol.

Point de Bruges was the name given to a lace made in and about that historic old town. This much resembles Malinese lace, but the arabesques of its designs were outlined with several fine threads, instead of one coarse thread; and flowers, filled in with open work, were introduced with pleasing variety. This lace, which was very fine and sheer, was also made in silk, and its width did not usually exceed three to five inches. Like the Antwerp lace, it was used chiefly for cap trimmings.

Point de Paris. This is the name by which is known the exquisite pillow lace made in the vicinity of Paris during the eighteenth century. It is an extremely fine and dainty lace with beautiful garlands trailing over the tulle and edging the flounces. The tulle of this lace is called *"champ double,"* (double field), and its mesh is round and strong, though very fine and is produced by doubling the quantity of threads, using eight instead of four. *Point de Paris* is as fine in quality and execution as old Brussels lace, but it resembles in appearance the richest laces of Bruges.

Valenciennes Lace is known the world over wherever lace is used on linen. It is made with a solid square or diamond shaped mesh, that is platted with four threads four lines on each side. It has a somewhat stiff flower or arabesque border made in close stitch along the edge, which is finished off with purls. The antique *Point de Valenciennes* which was made at the French town of that name was the most perfect pillow lace ever manufactured

and of fabulous price. It is composed of the finest thread as yet
spun in Europe, valued at about $4,000 a pound, and is almost
indestructible. Some of the present, machine-made laces are
copied from the most graceful of these antique designs, which
much resemble those of *Point de Paris;* but the manufacture of
this lace in the town of Valenciennes itself, has ceased entirely.
The fabrics now sold under the name of Valenciennes are manufactured in Belgium, especially in the neighborhood of Ypres.
They are also produced in large quantities in Normandy and
other Provinces of France, in England and Ireland and in Naples.

"**Point de Lille,**" so-called from a town in northern France,
is a fine lace with an anology to that of *Malines* and also to certain
varieties of *Point d' Esprit.* The old English lace called New-
port-Paguel strongly resembles it.

"**Chantilly,**" is a silk or thread pillow lace, made with either
a coarse or a fine tulle ground produced without plaiting, by
simply twisting the threads together, and is strewn with close and
varied flower designs or conventional patterns surrounded by a
coarse thread; the English lace of Lyme-Regis somewhat resembles it though it is more ordinary. Since the revival of the manufacture of lace on a large scale in France every kind of silk or
thread lace is made, or its production abandoned, as fashion
dictates in the different lace centers of that country such as
Normandy, Brittany, Surillac, Auvergne, and la Tourraine. To
these productions modified by the prevailing fashion, the manufacturers give fancy names, so as to attract the attention of the
general public, which is known to prefer novelty to a strictly
beautiful although old-fashioned object. For an example, *Cluny*
which is so often quoted, has never existed as a distinctive lace.
No lace whatever has been manufactured within the memory of
man inside the walls which bear that name, for Cluny is an old
castle in the heart of Paris which has been turned into a Museum
of Industrial Art, and some clever manufacturer, having arranged
a fresh and effective combination in guipure inspired by specimens of the rare old *Genoese point* existing in the museum's rich
collection, gave this name to his production, so as to attract the
shopping public by means of that charm which clings to the

name Cluny, knowing that the word would conjure up the historical walls of the quaint castellated museum, and the memories of mediæval Paris, near to the heart of every well-to-do Frenchman. All narrow edgings were formerly called "*Passements*." The name originated in Northern Italy and passed into France where it was used until the seventeenth century as a general designation for what we call *lace* and *gimp*, although after that period it became confined to gimp trimmings. The most celebrated of the ancient passements were of *gold* and *silver* and *clinquant* (plated copper), and were made in France and Spain and Italy. The great centers, however, from which metal laces were shipped all over Europe were Genoa, Milan and Florence. Some of these were most sumptuous in appearance and of surprising width considering the costliness of the raw material. Frequently colored silk was mixed with the other threads to facilitate the execution and diminish the cost, without destroying the general effect.

"**La Bisette**" was a coarse, narrow heavy, unbleached lace, without any distinguishing characteristics, used by the middle classes in France and Belgium during the seventeenth century.

"**La Guense**," *beggar lace*, was a great favorite in 1700; it was also unbleached, but was sheer and narrow, with a coarse net ground and graceful pattern.

"**La Campane**" was a very fine, narrow, white or unbleached pillow lace, used for the edging of caps or broad strips of straight edged lace. In the Italian word "campane" (bells) is to be sought the origin of its name; because the teeth of which it is composed formed a bell shaped edge to all it trimmed.

"**La Mignonette**" is so called from "mignon" meaning small and graceful. This lace was also frequently called "*Thread Blonde*." It consists in a fine thread edging composed of light transparent meshes.

‘ **Blonde**" was originally a narrow lace, which took its name from the pale yellow or blond tint of the unbleached silk of which it was composed. The simplicity of this lace soon disappeared owing to the introduction of rich designs in bleached and dyed silks frequently varied by gold and silver threads. *Modern blonde* is more largely manufactured in France and Genoa than in Spain. It is a wide round-meshed, sheer silk lace, with designs composed of large, flat surfaces made in a close stitch, surrounded by a coarse silk thread. In the more ordinary qualities, the design is embroidered by hand upon machine-made silk tulle and then filled in by darning; it is also very easily imitated entirely by machinery and sold very cheaply. At one time *blonde* was extensively made in Venice, but this branch of industry has died out there since the revival in the production of thread lace and guipures at Palestrina. Genoa and Cantu are the actual centers of its manufacture in Italy, and our exhibit contains some beautiful modern specimens from the provinces of Liguria and Lombardy.

"**Point d' Esprit,** *Brittany Lace* or *Embroidered* or *Tambour tulle lace*," was made in large quantities in Devonshire, England, in Brittany and around Genoa, where its production continues. The bands of embroidered tulle which still trim the caps of the good wives in the little town of Tulle, in France, are made entirely by bobbins and have given their name to the round mesh ground of every variety of lace. Many very clever lace makers formerly spent their lives doing nothing else but producing with a marvelous perfection these patternless bands ready for other hands to embroider, but after the introduction of machine-made tulle its manufacture no longer furnished a means of livelihood, and the poor workers were forced to seek fresh occupations. On the band of tulle, known to commerce as "footing," is embroidered (in fine darning stitch) charming flowers with open-work hearts or small detached, conventionalized designs; the ground is also frequently strewn with little, embroidered dots, to which the lace owes the name of "*Point d' Esprit*," or "*Spirit point*" so often given to it. To complete the lace a coarse thread is drawn around the embroidery, forming an outline to the flowers and stems and leaves. The edges of the antique Brittany laces are left without ornamentation, although the modern qualities and machine-made varieties are generally ended off with scallops or teeth in a hole stitch. From it is copied the common embroidered cotton tulle made by machinery in enormous quantities that drugs the market and is very pretty for window curtains and furniture, although its use on clothes is decidedly inartistic

Punto di Milano, *Milanese point* and *Punto di Napoli, Neapolitan point,* are different names for a lace with round mesh ground, so named from the Italian cities of Milan and Naples which were the two great centers of its production. This lace has always been a favorite, as it washes well and is excessively strong, and its manufacture has spread to all the countries of Europe. It resembles Genoese pillow lace, having the same scrolls and flowers formed by a ribbon in close stitch, with a mesh or tulle ground, whereas the Genoese lace is held together by bars.

The *Neapolitan Point* has a much rounder mesh than the Milanese, but the character of the design is what most distinctly indicates in what part of Italy the lace was made. This same rule also applies to all Europe, for although in the coarser qualities the technicalities constituting a lace named after a special town were adopted as a standard for the same kind of lace produced in other places, in the finer varieties transplanting, even to the nearest village radically altered the quality of the lace.

Torchon Lace (literally dish cloth lace). Torchon is the French generic term by which the following ordinary pillow-laces used on personal and household linen, are commercially known *Wirthschafts-Spitze,* or household lace, is the name applied to it in Germany. *Merletto di Cantu di Palestrina, degli Abruzzi,* etc., is the name by which it is called in Italy, after the great centers of its production. It is an ordinary pillow-lace with a net ground, and is universally used on underwear, household and church linen; it is worked straight along like weaving without the assistance of a crochet needle, as in *Milanese Point* and in the Guipures—so that it is in reality the simplest and purest of bobbin laces. Its especial qualifications for general use are its great strength, variety of pattern in endless geometrical combinations and its low price.

Machine made imitation of torchon costs two-thirds the price of real torchon and is very easily torn, whereas the real torchon outlasts the garments on which it is placed and is therefore the cheapest pretty edging that is manufactured. Owing to the facility of communication and the exigencies of fashion the same designs are adopted in France, Belgium, Bohemia, Portugal, Ireland, England, India, Colombo, Saxony, Germany, and many other countries, as are made all over Italy. A few of the most distinctive varieties which may interest the reader here follow, those which coincide in design being placed together.

Dalecarlle, a Swedish bobbin lace resembles that of *offidea*, which is a variety of Italian lace that is made in the Province of the Marche, as well as the common *Abruzzi lace*. These laces are all worked without any drawing, the rude design being produced by skipping the pin holes in the geometrically perforated cardboard. The pattern thus produced is surrounded by a heavy thread and composed of a close stitch worked between the meshes of the coarse net ground.

Sometimes the heavy thread is left out, this work is the last remaining tradition of a most exquisitely fine pillow lace, which was made a century ago in these provinces. Lately in Sweden the manufacture of lace has been protected and the workwomen have been directed with loving care with the happiest results, whereas the workers in the Marche and Abruzzi are entirely neglected, although with a small capital in ready money and a little patience this industry could be revived with great profit to the capitalist and enormous benefit to the surrounding country which is excessively miserable and poor—the women being ready and willing to work but requiring instruction and direction.

Mediæval household lace, was made in most of the Spanish, Dutch, Danish, German and Italian provinces. It ended in a straight edged finished off with purls, and the design was often so thick with inter-laced patches of close work, that the net ground was almost or wholly suppressed so that it appears like drawn work executed in a fancy pattern upon coarse linen. The open work is left by twirling two or four threads several times together and by the holes in which the pins following the outline of the drawing have been pricked.

Reticella a Fuselli is a mediæval pillow lace which is an exact copy of the celebrated *Punto Greco*, *Punto Tagliato* and *Reticella*. In certain museums I have seen the finer examples placed and

classified with the needle laces which bear the above names, no
one having observed under the microscope the difference in the
execution of laces, and it was used extensively in household linen
with most happy effect to replace the above named more expensive and tedious points.

Madeira lace is composed of a close stitch without a regular
set ground which is instead formed of varied webs and open
spaces, and is varied by oriental wheel-like designs which are
very artistic and pleasing to the eye.

Ceylon laces, as also those from the Mediterranean islands
have a mediæval, charming effect sometimes resembling the
above, at others seeming counterparts of certain Maltese laces.

Sicilian Torchon has no design drawn upon the parchment.
The peasant lace-maker follows the dictates of her fancy, forming
bizare combinations of webs and nets by introducing the pin, or
skipping the holes which are punctured at regular intervals all
over the strip of parchment after it has been firmly sewed upon
the cushion or "balon." Sicily was formerly celebrated for its
gold and metal laces, but the production of these has nearly died
out; some philanthropic souls are now trying to organize and
procure a revival of this industry so as to give a means of support
to the women of Palermo and other populous centers. At
Messina many varieties of old Sicilian lace are reproduced with
great exactness.

At present every variety of fancy work receives its own distinctive appellation, and all the old stitches that enter into its
composition are decked out with new and attractive names and
in the past in the same way, the laces made in every town, ham-
let, castle or cottage, by young and old, rich and poor alike received especial denominations applied to the designs and,
stitches according to the dictates of the chief workwoman's
imagination.

Brief as is this introduction, it describes one hundred and
twenty-two of the principal kinds of lace and yet not a quarter
of the appellations by which these laces and their varieties are
known in different countries have been mentioned, although the
reader's patience and memory have already been severely taxed

Multiplying one hundred and twenty-two by four and the product by twenty (the average of nine thousand seven hundred and sixty) is produced, a sum representing the names of individual stitches, which, for brevity and to avoid tedium have been carefully suppressed.

Many laces, however, have forty or fifty different terms applied to their component parts, each given because of the introduction of some different stitch or combination, and the stitches composing even the narrowest torchons are six or seven in number so that the general average given above is very low— should one add the terms applied in different places to the material and implements employed in the manufacture of lace, the sum would become very long and wearisome and the enumeration of the terms would form a good-sized vocabulary. We have drawn attention to these figures simply that they may serve as a refutation to a general and erroneous impression common to many highly cultured people that *lace-making* is only worthy to be classed among the secondary industries instead of standing high among the textile and decorative arts which adorn our homes.

If this preparatory study has appeared long it has assumed its present form in order that the *History of Lace*, which follows and describes our exhibit at the Columbian Exposition, may not be full of wearying technicalities and voluminous notes.

We trust that the following chapters will justify the course adopted. If not, the fault lies in the inexperience of the narrator and not in the lack of interest and variety to be found in following through the ages the development of this graceful, refined and ornamental branch of *Industrial Art.*

PART II.

The Birth of the Textile Arts and the Origin of Lace.

Man loves ornament; had he existed when the earth was without form and void, it might have been different, for first impressions are indelible; but, when his mind opened to look about him and observe, ornament attracted his attention on every side. Cradled in the lap of a young world, he saw fair Nature robed in a many hued garment, covered with reliefs of shrubs and trees checkered by cunning traceries of branches and leaves and their shadows dancing in the sunshine. Her mantle was trimmed with open work borders of meadow-land, fretted with great patches of parti-colored flowers, while dainty fringes of interlaced ferns and grasses nodded on the edges of the silvery water courses. When the winter came Nature prepared to sleep and changed these robes for a white sheet of dazzling snow diversified with wondrous interlaced patterns worked by the magic touch of frost in ice and rime. Then for the first time man saw, mirrored in God's handiwork, the exquisite designs which in the future ages his descendants were destined to copy, producing lace. The mind of primitive humanity was, however, undeveloped as that of a young child and could not analyze the impressions received nor even realize their existence, and yet in making for itself rude coverings of skins and plaited grasses or utensils of bone, it copied surrounding objects groping darkly for that with which to adorn its possessions. When we look into the misty vistas through which wandered prehistoric man we find the traces of his footsteps on the rocky paths of the Stone age, marked with curious carvings of zigzags curves and animal designs.

Nature, well pleased at the compliment paid her in these early efforts, covered them over with dust and earth, hiding them away until the time when mankind should be so developed as to appreciate the value of these records of his past, just as a fond mother after long years, draws from some private recess a carefully treasured object, rudely executed, and shows it to her grown-up son, to prove to him, how clever he already was at the time he thinks he must have been only a stupid, useless burden on her care.

At the earliest moment of his existence, man must have felt the necessity of some means by which to snare birds and beasts and fish for food, and observing how they were sometimes caught in the tangled weeds and thickets, he invented the twisting of grasses and fibres into ropes, which when knotted rudely together formed primitive nets.

Naturally, the first ornaments for the person and attire were the trophies of prowess such as boar's teeth, tusks, etc., worn strung together as necklaces, bracelets, etc., and on the garments they consisted in fringes formed by the long hair of furs. These all served as the models from which were copied the first trimmings on rude textiles.

The Lake Dwellers.

In Europe, the earliest race of which we know anything definite is that of the *Lake Dwellers*, whose industries are most interestingly illustrated by the fragments of their utensils, which are found in the great bogs and lakes of Switzerland. They existed from the time of the Troglodites through the Stone and far into the Bronze age, some say even into the Age of Iron, although they became extinct before the invasion of their country by the Romans. .

In *Asia* we find the earliest artistic, ornate textiles among the Assyrians and the Indians, and in *Africa*, among the Egyptians, but as the foundation of Art (as we understand the term) and the unbroken chain of evidence in regard to its history is to be found in their monuments and sepulchers, we will examine the Stone age in Europe first as illustrated by *Lake Dwellers*, and then turning to Assyria and Egypt for instruction, only leave them when their arts have accomplished the civilization of the peninsulas of Europe and the northern coast of the Mediterranean.

One can understand that in the dry atmosphere and sand of Egypt, delicate objects like textiles would resist the wear and tear of centuries; although marvelous, it must ever seem to touch objects produced by human skill thousands of years ago; but it is nothing short of a miracle that beneath the peat and mud and slush, frozen and thawed alternately for ages beyond the memory of man, such perishable things as cords and stuffs made of a curious flax developed from the wild variety which is native to the west coast of the Mediterranean, prepared and spun as it would be by a peasant of today, have remained to give us proofs—meager though they must perforce be—of this early race of Europeans. Besides the baskets that were most artistically woven of bark, fibre or sedges, and the fishing nets made of coarse linen or fibre twine knotted into as regular meshes as if produced today, especially interesting for our branch of study are the remnants of stuffs, and the bone, horn and bronze needles and crochet hooks used for making nets and knotting fringes into the edge of the textiles.

Samples of all these objects are exhibited on the *Revolving screen*, which serves to illustrate through them the origin and history of lace, whilst the voluminous objects are placed around the walls in the glass cases nearest to the screen.

Nos. 1 A and 1 B are illustrations made from textiles found at Robenhausen by Herr K. Forrer and Herr H. Messikommer and are taken by kind permission of the authors from an interesting pamphlet on the subject of Lake Dwellings published by them, and entitled *Prehistorische Varia aus dem Antiqua*, special Zeitschrift für Vorgeschichte, Zurig, 1889.

No. 67 represents a twisted hank of flax.

No. 74 represents a skein of twine.

No. 63 represents a tassel made of twine.

No. 70 represents a piece of rope.

Nos. 68, 69, 73 and 75 represent basket work of woven sedges, straw and woody fibre.

Nos. 59, 60 and 61 represent different qualities of net.

Nos. 62 and 71 represent textiles, with and without selvedge.

Nos. 72 and 73 represent embroidered textiles.

Nos. 94 **and** 65 represent textiles edged with fringes; though this variety is not reproduced here; these fringes were frequently twisted together and knotted at the ends.

No. 70 A represents a textile with passementerie fringe.

No. 1 C is a real piece of the coarse basket plaiting found in Robenhausen.

No. 1 D contains two bits of loom-woven textiles from Robenhausen.

When Herr Messikommer's father found the first fringed stuff at Robenhausen in 1857, he showed it to an expert, who said it was modern Paris passementerie work, but soon some other pieces were found in the same excavations and in the midst of surroundings which furnished positive proofs of their authenticity as work of the ancient Lake Dwellers.

Simple but practical weavers' frames, thread and twine, which serve now for sewing sails, up to the dimensions of large cords, have been found in skeins or already worked into stuffs, nets, tassels or fringes; also a peculiar, very strong material, plaited instead of woven out of course twine, has been found which might have served as a kind of sail cloth.

At Ingenhausen in 1882 were found the embroideries illustrated on the screen—the designs of which may have served as models for the perfected ornaments of the Bronze age. The rarity of these objects is explained by their only being found among the remains of dwellings destroyed by fire in windless weather, combined with circumstances which would cause inflammable stuffs to drop into the water uncharred, when the floor beneath them and the roof above were reduced to the fine, close-packed ashes adapted to preserving textiles from destruction by insects or by the waves. To form a better idea of the men and women among the Lake dwellers we must look for the race, which at present best illustrates the savage life of the past, and, allowing for the influences of climate and contact with the Arabs, and the Europeans, it appears that Central Africa can furnish the information we desire.

Card II, A, B, C, D Screen.

Card II shows four sketches of savage dwellings.

A II represents a Lake Dwellers' settlement, reconstructed according to the opinion of one of the most eminent professors of archaeology.

B II represents a *granary* of the Babusesse tribe as illustrated in Henry Stanley's latest work on Africa.

C II represents part of a Bongos village in Africa

D II represents a group of Lake-dwelling aborigines in New Guinea.

The Africans use boats hollowed out of trees as did the Lake-dwellers, their pottery has the same ornamentation and is baked in the sun as was that of the Lake dwellers; they live in settlements instead of following a nomadic life, and have many other customs in common, therefore in studying their rude arts and divisions of labor, we may hope to ascertain much about the daily life of the Lake dwellers at the time of their greatest development. All through the interior of Africa and in the basins of the Upper and the Lower Agowe and the Congo the woman does all the hard work, while the man reserves to himself what might be called the amusing *occupations*. He goes to the two big fishing reunions that are held every year at the time when the water in the great rivers is at its lowest, he snares birds and animals for food and clothing, he goes out to the hunts and battles, to war and to plunder, and thoroughly enjoys the excitement of this life, whilst the woman remains at home and busies herself in a modest daily round that is startling in its fatiguing variety. Besides the care of the children and of the domestic animals, she does all the field and farm work, cultivates the cereals, cuts the wood and fishes along the smaller streams. She gathers up and carries on her back all the products of her labor, and the fruits from the plantations that are often at great distances from the village; arrived at her home she helps to tidy up the village, and then instead of retiring she grinds the flour, cooks the meals and still finds time to weave artistic palm mats and sheetings and to *model* and to *bake* the simple pottery that is needed for domestic use.

The smiths and the weavers of fine "rafia" cloths are only

men especially apprenticed to a trade, who remain always faithful
to their tools.

The industries in which savage man *indulges*. When at home,
for he never *works*, are the making of fishing and hunting nets,
the sewing together with great neatness of the squares of rafia
produced by the professional weavers. The making of *"puka"*
(or bags) in fine needle work, ornamental carving, and the
shaping and polishing of the wooden parts of weapons. When
necessary he also attends to the construction of pirogues and
huts, the only two of all these occupations that are really hard
work.

Card III contains two pen and ink sketches that were made
on the back of an English cotton goods label by my late brother-
in-law, Giacomo di Brazzà, who spent several years traveling in
Africa with Cavaliere Peule, on an expedition of research which
was commanded by his brother, the celebrated African explorer,
Pierre de Brazzà, actually governor of the French Congo.

III 1 is a sketch of a wig or hat worn by a Bataké chief; it
is composed of fringes and cords in pineapple fibre, dyed black,
and knotted like the above-mentioned " Parisian passemente " of
the Lake dwellers.

III 2 represents a fringed square of woven rafia (of the
natural color of raw silk), such as is worn by the Bataké as a
kind of cap or head-handkerchief.

No. IV is a piece of rafia with knotted fringe, which has
been placed in the glass cases with the following voluminous
pieces of African lace kindly lent by Cavaliere Peule.

No. 5 is a *"puka"* (bag or pocket) made with the needle in a curious, complicated lace stitch. These pockets are
everywhere used in the Upper and Lower Ogowe and in many
parts of the Congo country; the band or handle is slipped over
the arm and shoulder-blade with the bag hanging underneath the
arm-pit, and these sacks serve as pockets as well as traveling bags
in that land where clothing is too scant to furnish a fold in which
to tuck away the smallest object. They are more or less ornate,
according to the fancy of the artificer, and a self-respecting
Agowean would not be found without one in his possession if he

could make, buy, borrow or steal it. Our particular "puka" is the
work of a member of the Abomba tribe, which is also distinguished for its tonsorial artists.   These produce marvelous effects
with the pates of their fellow-citizens, for they *plait* and clip and
shave the woolly hair into most complicated and ornate head-
dresses adorned with gew-gaws, and bisected with little shaved
lines and spots which meander among the knobs of wool and
cause their heads to resemble relief maps of their own dark continent.   But to return to the puka exhibited, which is very com-
modious, elastic and decidedly stylish, with its adornment of
elephant bristles and the large iron bell that has charmed the
tedium of many a long journey with its clatter; these pockets
are made of fine twine manufactured from the leaves of the pineapple plant.   The workman cuts the leaves into strips about half
an inch in width and passes these between his thumb and a sharp
knife, thus most daintily removing all the leafy part that covers
the fibre of the plant; then he rolls the fibre into a fine double
twine a couple of yards in length by rubbing it carefully with the
palm of his hand on his leg above the knee until it becomes perfectly smooth and even; this twine he threads into a needle and,
beginning the bag at the small end, he works spirally, widening
when necessary, first with a double button-hole stitch and afterward with one much more complicated, until the whole is completed of one continuous thread; to avoid knots, every time the
worker's allowance of twine is nearly exhausted he unthreads the
needle and splices the end of the twine with fresh fibre, rolling it
into a fine twine as before upon the flat of his knee, and continues
repeating the same operation every time fresh thread is required
until the bag is finished

One may imagine that these articles are not completed in a
day.   Cavaliere Peule told me that, on an exploring expedition
he once observed a denizen of a certain village on the Upper
Ogowe working industriously on one of these bags.   Returning
to the same place six months later he found the same villager
sitting at the same spot, and working on the same bag, which
was still far from being completed.   An African in his native
wilds is never over industrious—therefore the friends and advo-

cates of limited labor and fresh air for the **working classes need**
have no fear that during the time which **elapsed between Cava-**
liere Peule's two visits this man **did not enjoy sufficient exercise,**
recreation and sleep.

No. 6 is **a** gem in more ways **than** one, for **it is** not only
considered locally very valuable and is worn by the chiefs on the
shores of the Loanga as a badge of office, but it is *real lace, made*
with a needle, and the stitches of which it **is** composed are **the**
counterpart of those **in** the beautiful *Punto in Aria* of Venice.
It is a cap of **the same** form as a Phrygian, **or a** Neapolitan fisherman's cap; **special** attention should be given to its shape, as
much will be said in **the** following pages about this particular
head gear, which is gradually becoming obsolete. The fabrication of this African cap begins at the center of the crown with a
tiny but perfect wheel, which is increased by alternate open and
close stitches of exceeding fineness, made with perfect regularity
of spacing and depth; at intervals diamonds are formed of close
work, alternating with a ground of open stitch, **and the** completed cap is finished off with a band at the edge **which is** produced in quite a different kind of stitch. The thread used is fine,
strong and pliable, resembling unbleached flax or hemp, but is
not of the same construction as these, when examined under the
microscope. Might not this be the fibre used by the Lake
Dwellers which scientists have failed to classify, and which has
successfully resisted the wear of centuries? Leaving the savage
races to search among those of known civilization, we may go
back for centuries upon centuries without finding the origin of
textiles. The ancient monuments of Babylonia and Assyria fur-
nish the names of kings who reigned three thousand five hundred
years before Christ, living to the great age of the early patriarchs,
and some of these princes must have existed near the time of the
flood, as frequent allusions are made on their **inscriptions to** that
awful calamity.

In studying **the history of the world as** depicted on the monuments of **Egypt, the exodus of the** Jews appears a trivial bit of
modern history; **and Abraham's visit** to that country, during
which his pretty young wife Sarah, attracted great attention at

court by her beauty, grace of manner and accomplishments, seems a romantic episode in the life of an ancestor. The Egyptian hieroglyphics which represent long lines and dynasties of kings majestically arrayed, go back so very far that we lose our awe for the book of Manin, the Ramayana and the Mahabharata, which describe the civilization of India; the Illiad and the Penteteuch seem works of national history, and we look upon the book of Job, written two thousand five hundred years before Christ, as a comparatively modern classic. Whether the Egyptian and Assyrian races were twin sisters, or which was the first created, we can not tell, but both bear marks of the same Semetic parentage in lineage and character. In any case the stock was prolific, and a branch of it passed into India in the vanguard of the Aryan race, which, when the ground had been well cultivated by its industrious forerunners, in its turn emigrated and commingling its richer, more fiery blood with that of its predecessors gave a fresh incentive to all the arts of peace and war. These old nations were full of inventive knowledge, which it has been the fate of our modern civilization to rediscover and classify, for they even realized the existence of microbes although ignorant of the means adapted to destroying them, and so the Pantheistic religion of the Romans included special exorcisms and prayers addressed to their personification of a god. We will take Job as an example of ancient civilization in his exquisite poem, we receive the story of his life and experiences from his own lips, while Homer but repeats and idealizes what he has heard from others. Job was a rich Aryan chief or king. He possessed a palatial residence constructed of baked brick, having a portico adorned with columns. This dwelling was furnished with couches and beds, and with tables on which his meals were served on gold plate. At night the apartments were illuminated by means of oil lamps and candles. Utensils of copper, iron and earthenware, as also bottles made of skins, and sacks—cloth bags —served for the baser domestic uses.

Job lived in or near a city, for he speaks of the princes covering their mouths in token of respect when he passed them in the gate, and of the nobles and old men rising to do him homage and

waiting to be spoken to with the same courtesy that is now shown
toward rulers. He wore a diadem or crown of gold, gold earrings and a flowing robe edged about the neck with a collar.
This garment was girded with a leather or embroidered belt, and
over it he wore a rich mantle hanging from his shoulders. He
had also a mirror in which to admire his toilet when completed.
The garments he describes were carefully fashioned and sewed,
and the cloth which composed them was dyed of various hues
and woven of thread spun from flax, wool, camel's hair, and perhaps even silk. This is not certain, however, for although a _true_
legend ascribes to him a knowledge of the use of silk, it can not
be proved. In summer the woolen stuffs were packed away in
chests with strong-smelling woods and spices to save them from
destructive insects, as is also so well described by Homer centuries later. The treasury contained fine gold of Ophir, gold dust,
jewels of fine gold, gold coins, alloyed silver, sapphires, rubies,
crystals—by which term perhaps diamonds are meant—pearls,
onyxes, coral and Ethiopian topazes. The city in or near which
he lived had gates and walls, and was surrounded by a moat.
His fields were laid out with landmarks, fences, hedges and
ditches; he rented additional fields from his neighbors, and employed a thousand yoke of oxen to till his land. He had one
wife, who lived with him, while his three daughters and seven
sons had each a separate home; his own household consisted of
hired servants and slaves. The prisoners taken in war were also
in his time used as slaves and compelled to do the hardest work
including the building of great monuments, which princes caused
to be erected during their lifetime, to be sure of having worthy
mausoleums adorned with laudatory inscriptions carved in stone
or traced on terra cotta tablets. Books were written with iron
pens, and may have been composed of tablets or of rolls of palm
or papyrus, or possibly of leather, like the old Jewish bibles, since
there were boots, bridles, slings and water-bottles all made of
tanned skins. Job speaks of swift ships, of the phenomena of the
sea, the forces of nature, the condensation of rain and the purify-
ing effect of frost; he is also well acquainted with astronomy and
natural history, for he mentions the North star and the Pleiades,

and minutely describes the whale, the elephant, the camel, the
ox, the ass and the horse, as also sheep, goats, fowls, ostriches
and innumerable wild birds and animals. He occupied himself
with commercial as well as agricultural pursuits, and had scales
for weighing the merchandise. He sent out couriers and tax-
gatherers, and was so frequently visited by travelers and merchants from different countries that he kept interpreters in order
to be able to converse with them; he also was himself a traveler,
and when on a journey or on a hunting expedition made use of
tents for himself and his vast retinue. In his time there were
judges and physicians, and horse and foot soldiers, organized in
troops under officers, and furnished with iron and steel shields
and breastplates, and armed with swords, pikes, lances, slings,
and bows with flint heads for the arrows and sharp stones for the
slings—remnants of the usages of the stone age—are mentioned.
For hunting and fishing he possessed, in addition to the above-
named weapons, traps, snares, nets made of cord, hooks and har-
poons. He and his children were very hospitable, and gave frequent feasts which sometimes lasted late into the night, and to
which they invited not only their neighbors but also guests living
at great distances. The food was cooked and seasoned with salt,
olive oil, butter and milk; it consisted of meat, fowl, eggs and
vegetables, bread and cakes, made of corn, wheat or barley
ground between two stones into flour by the women; nuts, fruits,
honey and cheese came in later, as delicacies. The usual bever-
age at these banquets was wine made from grapes.

Job's religion was monotheistic; and though the sun and
moon were worshipped in his neighborhood, idols of wood or
stone had not yet become a part of the religions known to him;
all these details have been mentioned to prove how little certain
oriental races have altered in their customs since the oldest historic epoch, until in the last fifty years the penetration of European customs into the east produced innovations.

No poet, singing the heroic deeds of his nation would inter-
rupt the flow of stately verse to introduce trivialities which would
mar the completeness of his ode, or retard its climax, but sometimes when describing fair women and their attractions, the

ancient authors lingered lovingly over their charms and even added a description of the personal adornments which enhanced their loveliness, and these brief word-pictures coincide with the cartoons on Egyptian and Assyrian monuments, and Etruscan vases and tombs; whilst in the secluded homes of Indian princes this type of womanhood is still preserved. Graceful female forms are there still veiled with gauzy materials and robed in richly spangled tissues or draped in cunningly wrought mantles, embroidered along their hems with divers colors and trimmed with rich and complicated fringes, while about their pretty feet and arms, bangles and bells tingle as they move, busied with their household duties, or raise the curtains that veil the doorways of their apartment to catch a glimpse of the great world outside. These curtains are made of rich carpets or heavy materials adorned with intricate designs wrought in needle-work by themselves or by the maidens under their skilled direction.

But if we wish to touch and examine the very same flexibles which are mentioned by Homer and his contemporaries we must turn to the tombs in Egypt. The Egyptians believed in the bodily resurrection of the dead, and therefore caused the bodies of the departed to be carefully embalmed with spices and bitumen. This, combined with the dry atmosphere, many wrappings and numerous superposed mummy cases has preserved the rich garments in which the remains were clothed so that the beloved might not have to blush because of his mean attire on appearing before Osiris and the shades of the other world. Besides this the Egyptians adorned the walls of the tomb with drawings which were illustrative of the occupations and past life of the deceased, which were absolutely truthful in every detail, however simple and uneventful had been his existence, and generally showed also the number and employments of his servants.

The following illustrations are reproductions of some of these cartouches which, together with the information regarding them, we owe to the kindly interest taken in our work by Prof. Schioparelli, of the Egyptian museum, in Florence, while the collection of textiles, without which this exhibition would be incomplete, is due to the well-known antiquarian author and critic, Herr R.

Forrer, of Strassbourg. I therefore gladly avail myself of this opportunity for heartily thanking them both in the name of our committee and in my own for the valuable information they have contributed to this little book, and for the benevolence and patience with which they replied to our frequent importunings.

Nets were made in Egypt in great abundance, and from the remotest times; the process of their manufacture is pictured in No. XIV A, on the tomb of the feudal prince *Nekira*, near Beni-Hassan, in Upper Egypt, which was decorated during the twelfth dynasty, about 2500 B. C. The same design (with slight variations, which prove it no copy), is repeated one thousand years later on a tomb of the seventeenth dynasty near Thebes. No. XIV B shows two ways of snaring birds with nets, and is from the same tomb as also is XIV C, which indicates that the Egyptians, like many savage nations, and like the American and Asiatic Indians, used nets for carrying heavy weights. The cartouch XIV C represents a water-carrier with two jars, borne in nets. It will be observed that in the manufacture of these nets instead of using a bifurcated needle the two workmen employ balls of twine and shuttles or spindles, and that the net is stretched on a horizontal frame, being worked at both ends at once. These large nets were made of flax or cotton twine and were used alike for bird catching and for fishing as well as for curtains in the doorways and windows of houses to exclude the flies and other insects which swarm in that country at all seasons of the year.

No. XV is a much older illustration of the use of nets than the preceding cartouche and is taken from a bas relief in the tomb of the dignitary, Tebchmi, near the great pyramid constructed under the rule of the fifth dynasty, 3300 B. C. It represents a man carrying a pole on which are hung several bird cages. Just as on any autumn morning one may see an Italian bird snarer carrying his decoys to the trimmed thickets where his nets are spread. There are many monuments older than the above which also illustrate the use of nets in Egypt.

No. XVI, screen, is a drawing which represents a fine net, which exists in the Egyptian museum at Florence; it is of twine, rubbed with bitumen and is also evidently made for catching birds or small fish, as it is composed entirely of little, close set bags of net in which the game, once it has entered, must perforce remain suspended, without power to move or escape, that resembling in its effect the fine silk net left loose between two coarser ones at present used for bird catching in Italy. In the Florentine museum there is another net made entirely of leather, in which material slits are regularly cut close together on the same principle and with like effect as our Christmas tree nets for sweets clipped out of silver paper. These leather net-like curtains must have served in the doorways and windows of the wealthy, or perhaps to save animals from being tormented by flies and gnats as nets are now thrown over horses in summer in warm climates, with the same object in view.

No. XVII represents a little, double-knotted bag which was made to hold a porphyry balsam bottle. It is most artistically worked in macrame stitch and resembles in effect the meshes of the celebrated *reseau double,* on double ground of old Burano lace. On Greek and Etruscan vases we find the reproduction of nets in endless variety, but nothwithstanding their universal use for domestic purposes, we have no proof that they were adopted as ornaments *embroidered* to adorn clothing, although many of the elaborately knotted fringes of the Egyptians, Assyrians and Jews produce the effects of nets. *Fillets* were in general use among the Greeks and Etruscans for binding up the hair, and were worn with diadems, and with or without veils. They are often represented as ornamented with designs, but we can not tell whether these represent gold buttons, or embroidery or filagree work, for in the decorations on the vases the treatment is somewhat conventional.

In No. VIII A are shown some Greek costumes photographed from the famous Sysipha vase in the museum at Munich. The earliest Egyptian mummy cloths are like those of the Peruvian mummies, almost prehistoric, and have the same weaving and texture as the stuffs of the Lake Dwellers. We have no illustrations of these, but No. XVIII A will serve our purpose, though it is of a later period from Achminë Panopolis. In it the warp threads are left as a fringe, and No. XVIII B shows how, after working an inch or two of texture, the woof was drawn out or omitted, so as to form a transparent border. This ornament was at other times varied by spaces of open work, as in No. XVIII C, in which the weft is shot across behind the warp at regular distances, for a certain number of threads, and then the ordinary weaving continues, thus forming alternate squares. The woof threads were then cut away if desired. At a later period these open spaces were filled in with colored embroidery.

No. IX, screen, represents a skirt embroidered round the belt and arranged with braces to support it from the shoulders.

No. XII, screen, is a design that dates from an inscription belonging to the dynasty which reigned 2,500 years before Christ, and is preserved in the museum at Florence.

The early Egyptians also made fringes which were knotted into the material they were destined to adorn, or sewed on afterward. We find frequent examples of garments trimmed with these on sashes and on the edge of skirts, as also deep fringes worn about the neck; when this is the case the women thus adorned are frequently represented as engaged in menial service or manual labor which indicates the lower classes who may have adopted this fashion in imitation of the rich necklaces of their betters and to satisfy their love of color and ornament at small cost. These neck-fringes remind one of the artistically plaited grass necklaces made and worn by the wild tribe of Matheran in northern India and the work of these is the same as that which served as a model for the beautiful oriental gold necklaces found in the Etruscan tombs, and which are still executed without variation by the artisans of India, who cling with loving faithfulness to the traditions of their ancestors despite the innovations of the nineteenth century.

The bas-reliefs executed in honor of the princes belonging to the nineteenth and twentieth dynasties on the royal tombs in the valley of the Kings near Thebes, furnish us with many illustrations of elaborate fringes. No. X, screen, represents queen Tarhat, mother of Pharoah Amonenses, on whose tomb she is portrayed and who reigned in the thirteenth century before Christ. No. XI, screen, represents Queen Isit, wife of Rameses VI, as she is depicted on her own tomb. She belonged to the twentieth dynasty of the twelfth century before Christ. No. XII, screen, represents Rameses VII and No. XIII, screen, his wife, both copied from his tomb of the twentieth dynasty B. C. 1200.

No. XXXVI A, B and C, screens, are illustrations also taken from the royal tombs at Thebes. No. XXXVI A, represents an Arab chief of the Absha tribe which emigrated into Egypt during the twelfth dynasty, about 1600 B. C. No. XXXVI B, represents Arabs of the same tribe.

No. XXXVI C represents the Phœnician prince(*Hafa*) bringing gifts to a Pharaoh of the eighteenth dynasty, about 1900 B. C. The garments of this prince are beautifully worked and trimmed with fringes, cords and tassels. A correct idea of the princely and priestly clothing used in Egypt at the time Moses wrote his laws and the history of the ancestors of his race (about 1500 B. C.), may be obtained by reading the instructions given in Exodus xxviii, and the following chapters for the fashioning of the Jewish priestly garments, which were copied with modifications from those of the royal princes who at that period in Egypt were considered as belonging to the hierarchy of religion as well, and so had a double hold upon the superstitious populace; and it was in this capacity that Moses acquired much of his erudition and his knowledge of sanitary laws. The costume of the Jewish high priest, according to the regulations laid down by the greatest of the prophets, consisted first of an under-robe, or shirt, long and full in the skirt with sleeves to the wrist, worn over a pair of breeches, both of these garments being made of white linen; over the robe was worn the ephod or tunic of *"fine twined linen,"* an expression which in the light of modern erudition is considered incorrect, the Hebrew term translated, twined linen, being the same as that used elsewhere for silk. The ephod was therefore probably made of spun silk dyed blue; it was scant in the skirt and reached only to the knee; it had short sleeves and was bound about the neck with a piece of the same material, that it might not be torn in putting it on, nothing imperfect being allowed to approach the mercy seat This binding was beautified by an embroidered border in gold, purple and scarlet, with button-hole

4

stitch around the edges and around the openings, through which
the golden chains supporting the magnificent breast-plate and the
blue lace attaching it to the embroidered girdle were passed;
upon each shoulder an onyx stone engraved with the names of the
twelve tribes of Israel was set in rich embroidery, and the hem of
the ephod was adorned with a deep border, repeating the designs
upon the shoulders and about the neck, and was edged with a
fringe composed of alternated pomegranates made in blue, purple
and scarlet needle-work and small gold bells, which tinkled as he
walked, warning the devout of the high priest's approach. Upon
his head he wore a fine linen veil, or kerchief, edged with embroidery and fringe called the mitre, such as we see constantly in the
reproductions of Egyptian designs, covering the ears and hanging
down to the shoulders at the back; over this mitre the pharoahs
and the gods and goddesses of Egypt wore a winged crown, the
priests and princes a golden diadem marked with their arms, and
the Jewish high priest was ordered to have his made of a plate of
pure gold and engraved like a signet with the words "Holiness
to the Lord," and to have it attached upon his forehead by a blue
lace which passing to the back around the head was tied in a bow
and the ornamental ends allowed to hang down over the mitre.
To complete this regal costume a large and ample cloak or coat,
made of fine embroidered linen, was thrown over the shoulders.
From this description it is to be inferred that two kinds of work
not embroidered in the stuff were executed on these garments—
one being the pomegranates in colored silks, that being around the
edge of the ephod between the bells, and which would coincide in
design and treatment with Turkish needle-lace of the fifteenth
century after Christ, and the blue lace used to attach the breast-
plate and diadem made of silk and thread that was knotted
together like a passementerie or macrame bobbin lace. Cotton
was never highly esteemed for textiles in Europe, Africa and
Asia Minor during classic times, and it is first mentioned in the
Bible in the Book of Esther, though it must have been in use in
the far east for centuries before, and has always been particularly
appreciated by the Indians and Chinese. The occupations of the
Jewish women, the trust placed by the men in their advice, the

selection made from among them of rulers and judges, their erudition and literary accomplishments, their direction of the house and their management of the slaves and of home industries, their simple amusements and their intelligent devotion to the rearing of the children, all resemble these characteristics as portrayed in the lives of the most chaste class of Greeks and Etruscan matrons, who by their education, grave responsibilities and retired mode of life became most serious and philosophic, and were thus prepared to receive the teachings of Christianity and render staunch and valuable assistance and advice to the disciples of that religion from the first instant of its existence. The costume they wore was suited to their lives and occupations, and so preserved one type for centuries, and slightly modified by climate and nationality is that of the women of the early church until the eighth century after Christ.

On the other hand, the style of garments suited to the more enervated life and looser morals of India, Syria and Egypt was adopted by the gay-hearted dancing girls and the less sedate women of the Roman court, where fashions were as changeable as in Paris today. A matron's costume consisted of a flowing under tunic, or stola, with either long or short sleeves, as preferred; this was composed of heavy or light material, as fancy or the season might dictate. Over the stola a shorter tunic was worn, made full at the neck or of one straight piece clasped on either shoulder and draped across the breast. At the waist the garments were held in place by a belt of metal, leather or passementerie, or else by a simple ribbon. The feet were protected by shoes, slippers or sandals, to which stockings, bifurcated at the toe to admit the sandal strap, were added in winter. When walking abroad, and also at home in chilly weather, the matron wore a full toga edged with embroidery, or fringed or scalloped around the borders. A long veil consisting of a transparent material, more or less richly fringed or embroidered according to her wealth and the position she occupied in the social scale, was artistically draped over her hair and caused to hang down over her shoulders, often to the ground. The draping of this veil, and the combing of the hair beneath it, was considered of great im-

portance, and a diadem and any quantity of pins, fillets, ribbons
and jewels were used to adorn the locks, which were braided,
waved, curled or frizzed, quite in modern fashion.

Blind Homer, in wandering from palace to palace, must have
heard this branch of the feminine toilet freely discussed, for he
describes it precisely as we see it reproduced on Greek vases
adorned with representations of historical women, for instance.
In describing Andromache's grief he says:

 " Her hair's fair ornaments; the *braids* that bound;
 " The *net* that held them, and the *wreaths* that crowned;
 " The veil and diadem threw far away," etc.

Besides the golden wreaths which encircled her Greek knot
and the jeweled hair-pins which held her veil in place, the rich
patrician had innumerable brooches, rings and bracelets, clasps
and earrings, as well as chatelaines, composed of quantities of
tiny chains, to which were suspended all the objects that could
possibly be of use to rearrange her toilet when far from home, or
else those required in her household occupations. The gleaming
fillet or *net* that covered her hair was often composed of precious
metals, and was of complicated, exquisite workmanship like the
"golden net of Hephæstus"—whose texture e'en the search of
gods deceives—"fine as the filmy webs the spider weaves."
The young girls often allowed their hair to flow loose under their
veils or plaited it in long tresses, binding a simple ribbon or
gauzy net around the brows to hold the veil or hair in place.
They wore shorter and less ample tunics than the married
women, and no jewels but only a metal brooch of the simplest
pattern to clasp or pin together their garments wherever necessary. The Jewish men, who were neither athletic nor equestrian,
wore clothes very much like those of the women supplemented by a
coat with armholes instead of the toga. This coat was generally
dyed a dark color, and was freely adorned with fringes. The
men of Etruria, Greece and Rome had flowing robes for certain festivals and as badges of office, just as they had suits of armor for war;
but their daily costume consisted in the short, full tunic with or
without sleeves, belted in at the waist and covered by a toga that
hung majestically from the shoulders, or was wrapped about them

in studied folds so full or grace and dignity that they are still called *classic*. Sometimes the men adopted for riding and travel-ing, and in cold weather, a costume, arising perhaps from con-tact with the east, consisting of short breeches that were hidden beneath the plaits of a close-fitting tunic and a sort of cloth stocking or leggin strapped about with leather thongs coming from the leather slipper or low shoe, a fashion that is still fol-lowed by the mountaineers about Rome. They also had regular leather top boots, gauntlets and wallets. They wore helmets in time of war and on parade, but when following peaceful occupa-tions they made use of caps and fillets of a special form. No. XIX, screen, illustrates certain of these garments. No. XIX 1 repre-sents a tunic embroidered with *clavena* or stripes. No. XIX 2 is copied from a tunic embroidered with squares like those described as placed on either shoulder of the ephod ; both these drawings also illustrate the embroideries which were used on other parts of this garment.

No. XIX 3 screen represents a toga with *fringed edge ;* the toga and *pallium* are succeeded in these modern times by shawls, and by the blanket of the Red Indian. No. XIX 4 screen is a draw-ing of a knitted woolen bifurcated sock of mitten shape, thus made to allow the sandal-straps to pass on the inner side of the great toe and properly support the sole. No. XIX 5 represents a leather slipper. No. XIX 6 is a flat shoe of the hygienic com-mon-sense pattern, such as we should wear to-day were we not so wedded to tip-tilting French heels. No. XIX 7, screen, is a leather boot. The embroidered bands worn in the time of the early Roman empire on the tunic and the toga, as well as the fringes and borders still worn by the Jews at the same period, denoted by their size, form and color the rank and occupation of the wearer, and were established in the one case by imperial decrees, in the other by prophetic laws. Roman citizens alone were allowed to use the various shades of purple. The senator's distinctive ornament was a broad band or *claven*, which passing over the shoulder of the tunic descended before and behind, often reaching below the waist to the hem of the garment. The rank of knight was denoted by two narrow stripes of purple, the embroidered designs on the shoulders, a modification of which still remains in the Italian *cioceare* shirts used by the Roman peasants, of which one is exhibited, were often round or oblong instead of square, and then the pieces in the four lower corners of the tunic were shaped and designed to correspond with them; at other times the embroidery surrounding the hole left for the head to pass through, and which formed the neck trimming, was widened and made to descend several inches over the back and chest like a deep collar. Around the bottom of the richer tunic there was always a band of embroidery, or else one or more stripes were woven in the material of which it was made, or sewed on after it was completed. The tunic was made all in one piece, the opening for the head being left in the middle of the material during wearing, which was then sewn together on either side from the arm-pit to the hem. The toga for a full-grown man was about a yard and a half wide by two yards and a quarter long. It was often fringed or embroidered or woven with stripes at the ends or sides. At its corners there were also introduced rounds or squares of embroidery to match those on the tunic with which it was destined to be worn. The women of the latter empire wore graceful and exaggerated veils draped over the entire figure (instead of togas). This veil was called a *pallium*, and was made of thin, delicate material, embroidered or woven with fringes or borders, or scattered over with regularly recurring designs of flowers, leaves or birds, this kind being usually finished off with a fringe at the ends.

The garments of which we have been speaking are illustrated in the Italian Lace Exhibit by pieces of embroidery and textiles manufactured and worn by men and women in the manner above described during the first centuries of the Christian era. Such examples are very rare and were obtained from Herr. R. Forrer's unique collection of textiles, found in the necropolis of Achmin, a small city on the right bank of the Nile in Upper Egypt, which now consists of a population of about 30,000 inhabitants, of which number 1,000 are Coptic Christians, but in classic times was large, prosperous and celebrated under the name of Panopolis, and enjoyed an especial reputation during the Roman empire as a manufacturing center of costly stuffs and finely woven linens. The oldest graves lie about five feet below the level of the ground and often there are several sepulchres superimposed, which demonstrates the great antiquity of this burial place; in fact, it must have been used at least from the second century of our era until the time when Mahometanism had become predominant throughout Egypt. The graves consist of holes dug in the sand, in which the body was laid between boards, and they contain every imaginable article of the toilet, as well as the implements of various trades.

The stuffs found at Achmin consist in gauzes, silks, damasks and satins, made of pure silk or mixed with flax, woolens, linens and gobelin tapestries, and are striped, rainbowed, flowered, etc., by means of weaving, embroidery or stamping. The embroidery was executed on a ground formed in close textiles by leaving or drawing out the weft for a certain width, and in gauzes and muslins by pushing it apart. The design was embroidered upon the warp thus left with a coarse white thread.

No. XX, screen, is a water-color drawing from the Egyptian museum in Florence, showing part of a border worked in this way which had been sewn on a linen tunic, of which a piece still remains as foundation. No. XXII A screen shows a piece of the same work inserted into the material *on the bias*. Here we appear to be face to face with *Punto Girato* or *Reticella*, but alas! we soon discover that this resemblance is illusory and caused by the gnawing fangs of time which have eaten away the woolen *filling*, made in real gobelin stitch to form the ground, the white threads still existing only served to outline the design and to constitute a framework for dividing the colors.

No. XXII B screen represents XXII A before the gobelin stitch had been destroyed.

No. XXI screen shows us the wrong as well as the right side of a piece of finished embroidery.

No. XXIV screen represents a piece of embroidery or Gobelin of a later period when the white outlining had ceased to be used; the figures in this are roughly shaded precisely as in the tapestry made in the middle ages. The originals of the above articles date from the fourth to the seventh century of our era and we will now examine the real pieces of stuff.

No. XXV A screen is a medallion of embroidery which has lost nearly all the woolen filling, and therefore excellently illustrates the process followed in the fabrication of these trimmings. To accelerate the production of this elaborate work, the artisan made strips of belting of the desired width (notice the selvedge on the sides and raw edge of the ends) weaving a bleached woof into an unbleached twine warp, counting the stitches, and so leaving out a perfectly oval twine ground of the size and shape required on which the embroiderer could begin to work without wasting the time required for drawing the shreds out of a woven material. On the screen one corner of this example is turned over to show the wrong side of the work, and that the white outlining is executed in a kind of backstitch.

No. XXV B screen is the piece of a linen toga on which the above embroidery A was sewn when formed; in it are left the coarse threads which show that to keep the medallion from slipping while being secured to the material it was destined to adorn, it was basted across the middle in both directions and then overcast neatly around the edge, turning in the raw ends.

No. XXV C screen is part of a medallion of the same design, having evidently adorned the same toga, but in better preparation. The ground here is still filled in with red wool, and the white scrolls and circles with various colors. In the centre of this piece of work is the conventional little bust of Christ with a yellow halo on a black ground, and surrounded by a black border which is patterned in small crosses of red, green and yellow. This is early Byzantine work and is of the fifth century, as is indicated by the graceful scrolls in the design which still preserve a Roman character and are graceful despite the presence of the inartistic little bust. No. XXVI screen is the same kind of ornament introduced in very fine linen in a space left in the weaving, as in the unembroidered piece. No. XVIII B screen is more antique and artistic in design than No. XXV C, being work of the best Roman period. At that epoch embroideries were always made with a ground of solid color, generally black or one of the numerous shades of purple, with white outlining. This piece is probably a remnant of a woman's tunic manufactured about 300 A. D.

No. XXVII screen is of the same period as No. XXVI, but it is of coarser material and execution and may have formed part of the wide shoulder embroidery of a clovem trimmed tunic; its purple color denotes the Roman extraction or titular distinction of its wearer. No. XXVIII screen is part of a square of stuff woven at the same period but the ground is left of warp alone, the weaver having stopped the woof on each side when he reached the space to be embroidered, thus forming a selvedge. This piece seems to have formed part of a tunic, judging from the wrong side, which is too untidy, owing to the long threads hanging from it, for that of a toga. The outlining in this piece of embroidery was executed after the space had been filled in with the woolen ground. The stitches resemble those used in outlining Sicilian drawn lace.

No. XXIX screen is of the same period, it is a black border worked with equal neatness on both sides in a strip of warp left in weaving a fine linen toga. The design represents a grape vine with the white thread worked in before the introduction of the colored wool.

No. XXX screen is a piece of narrow border which is of more recent execution. The design is artistically drawn and represents a purple dog with red leading strings and tongue playing in a circle formed by two interlaced scrolls, the corners being filled with leaves of red or green. This border may have trimmed the toga of some child, for its effect is very youthful in contradistinction to that of all the other pieces in our collection.

No. XXXI screen and the two numbers following it date back at least to the fifth century. No. XXXI is coarsely executed in narrow stripes of dark ecru running at regular intervals along the length of the white etamine or cheese cloth material; between these stripes a basket of flowers is worked in parti-colored wools and without any white outlining. The basket is purple and is marked with yellow and white designs. The flowers are indicated by vermilion and white spots on a dark red ground surrounded by green leaves. This embroidery must have decorated a woman's toga or pallium and have been repeated at regular intervals along the border. No. XXXII A. B. and C. screens are the ends of scarfs consisting of their entire width, and belong to the seventh or eight century of our era. No. XXXII A ends in a fringe above which narrow stripes of red wool are introduced, after an inch of plain weaving in linen thread; then come six inches of plain weaving followed by two or three rows of fancy weaving and a space of four inches of warp left for the embroidered gobelin border. This border has a red ground which is framed on either side by a black stripe edged with yellow and dotted with little yellow squares at regular intervals. Three shields which may have been coats-of-arms are embroidered on the red band and are divided by rows of a kind of herring bone stitch in white and yellow silk; between these is repeated an oriental allegorical design representing the tree of life. The middle shield is adorned with a green parrot with yellow legs outlined in black and white, the other two contain white lions, outlined in black; everything is upside down showing in this work that the embroidery must have been done before the material was removed from the loom.

No. XXXII B screen is a scarf end of coarse muslin such as is in use to-day in the East. The design is embroidered in the same back stitch as is always found in the ordinary kind of Oriental reversible needle-work. Its discovery proved a treasure trove for our branch of textile art, for it has a needle-work border about the edge overcasting and ornamenting the hem which very much resembles modern Turkish work, and is the first example we possess of stitches similar to those used in modern oriental embroidery, as may be seen from a small, three-cornered piece which has been placed beside it.

No. XXXII C screen is woven in the same way as No. XXXII A, the embroidery is however worked in golden stitch and imitates the jewelled borders we see on the Byzantine mosaics of this period,

No. XXXIII A is a paralellogram of pure Gobelin tapestry sewed on a piece of fine linen and cunningly wrought with the

needle in divers colors. When new it must have been resplen-
dent for the design is most elaborate. In each upper corner of
this scrap there is a duck standing on its tail with its feet to the
right and its head to the left. In the middle of the design there
is a saint seated on a throne holding a sword in his right hand.
With the help of a lively imagination we discover also four green
and yellow dogs or lions seated on their haunches along the
lower border; two oblong bias strips placed at right angles to the
saint's neck and having narrow black borders spoked with yellow
are adorned with four ducks each, all in a row and standing on
their tails with their feet and toes carefully embroidered in mid
air to the right of their breasts. The visitor to the Italian
woman's section may not discover all these details for himself,
but it is well to know that they exist, as it shows the ludicrous
combinations which the debasement of drawing and its subser-
vience to the frenzy for colors was capable of producing at the
epoch of Byzantium's greatest supremacy.

No. XXXIII B screen is a piece of belting, both the warp and
the woof, in which are of a fine indigo color upon which is embroidered in white thread a conventional pattern by darning The
effect produced being that of the so-called "Alt Deutsch work,

No. XXX C screen is a red stripe darned into a coarse muslin
and evidently forming the border of a woman's garment. The effect obtained in the treatment of the design also has its counterpart
in the needle work of the fifteenth century in Europe; it is of particular interest with regard to the subject we are treating owing to
the fact that between the rows of darned work the warp of the
textile has been removed and the remaining threads caught
together by hemstitching, such as we use on the edge of our
handkerchiefs. The corners of these two samples are turned
over to show the work on the wrong side.

No. XXXIV screen is interesting because there are introduced, at regular intervals, stripes of quadruple woof; and
because the warp which has been made to take the form of birds
and tiny squares was not picked out, but was made to assume
these shapes in the weaving, and also because the fringe is hem-
stitched, just as it would be on an article manufactured today.

In No. XXXV screen we have the sheer material we call *gauze*, so often depicted on vases and monuments as forming the garments of goddesses and women of Greece, Etruria and Rome, some of which are reproduced among our designs.

Homer frequently mentions this gauze; thus, in Canto V of the Illiad:

> "And Pallas disrobes; her radiant veil untied,
> With flowers adorn'd with art diversified."

And in Canto VI:

> "The Phrygian queen to her rich wardrobe went,
> Where treasured odors breathed a costly scent;
> There lay the vestures of no vulgar art—
> Sidonian maids embroidered every part,
> Whom from soft Sidon youthful Paris brought
> With Helen, touching on the *Tyrian* shore.
> Here, as the queen revolved with careful eyes
> The various textures and the various dyes,
> She chose a *veil* that shone superior far
> And *glowed refulgent* as the morning star."

And in the Odyssey he describes this material as forming part of the costume of Ulysses:

> "Fine as a *filmy web* beneath it shone
> A vest that dazzled like a cloudless sun."

Lucian, in recounting the feast offered to Cæsar by Cleopatra, says that the Queen's costume consisted of "*a wondrous web of thin transparent lawn.*" This doubtless means a gauze embroidered in silk, like No. XXXV screen, which is unique, and represents two crested birds, executed in embroidery, such as is produced to-day in large quantities at Delhi and in other parts of India. The raw material may have been imported from that country, but Pliny records the tradition of the introduction of this kind of garment into Europe, and describes its manufacture in the island of

No. XXXVI is a gauze veil made in dark blue wool; it has a fringe composed of the twisted and knotted warp, and a white silk and red wool stripe forms the edge above this fringe. It is also adorned with several other stripes, which are woven in the material at regular intervals, and some of these are embroidered in letters and geometrical designs, with darned work in

white silk; so that what forms the relief on the right side constitutes the ground on the reverse, as in the belting described as
No. XXXIVC.

We have now reached the limit of close embroidery, or
embroidery without real open work in the design. We have
already met with hemstitching, and among the following examples in the glass cases near the African work there will be found
No. XXXVII B, a Turkish scarf belonging to Herr von Ugon. It
is about the same width as the scarfs No. XXXII A B C, and is
embroidered in silver, gold and shaded silks on a cotton muslin
ground; and the same stitches as in the Byzantine work will be
found in the hearts of the flowers, while the silver thread draws
together the light ground with the effect of Sicilian Point;
around the edge runs a scallop made in gold thread in button-
hole stitch, forming a regular needle lace.

No. XXXVII A, cases is a broader scarf, belonging to the same
exhibitor; it is of the same period but is much more complicated
in execution. Hungarian and Roumanian embroidery of the present day have preserved and developed the traditions recorded in
this piece of work. The lace about the edge is of a curious pattern, a kind of difficult macrame made with the needle No.
XXXVII cases also belongs to Herr von Ugon's collection and
is the artisque knee-covering made for a curious kind of
trousers formerly worn on the Island of Rhodes. The
colored embroidery on this piece of muslin has geometrical
designs in the style of No. XXXIV C, made in Sicilian stitch but
without the second, smaller stitch which is used alternately
and draws the ground together, forming the open work or
small çheckers, from which the tulle ground laces have
been evolved. Between the colored bands there runs a verit-
able Reticella, executed in white silk with the stitch of
which it is composed woven upon the threads left by drawing
out the woof, which is the same as that used in embroidering net
laces, and in making reversible gobelin embroidery so that
the varied openings and simple stitches of this narrow insertion
can serve to bridge the chasm which lies between the coarse close

gobelin ornaments executed in dyed wool and **the airy fabrics** of respected Venetian points and guipures.

No. XXXIX cases is a veil of antique embroidered muslin such, as Turkish ladies are in the habit of keeping within easy *reach* to throw quickly over their heads on the entrance of a visitor. This veil is a modification of the classic and more voluminous Talia, which, in its turn, had been evolved from the head covering used by the women in the time of Moses. The design of this piece is thoroughly Jewish or Assyrian in character, with its stiff trees and regular flower-pots disposed in conventional niches, with a minaret over each, wrought in fine reversible gold needle work, filled in with a silk ground of Sicilian Point. All along the edges of this veil hang pots of lovely silken rose bushes, alternated with baby yew trees worked in exquisite needle point without any foundation. Do not these blossoms, created by the needle, recall the purple and scarlet pomegranates that are described as hanging between the bells, at the bottom of Aaron's ephod? They are made on a narrow, black silk footing or passementerie, and afterwards sewed to the veil. The stitch in which they are worked is the same as that used in the Ogowe cap; they are essentially punto in Aria! They are real lace! This work is complicated in design and difficult of execution. It is still made in Turkey, and always imitates flowers, leaves and bell-shaped blossoms, buds or fruits. The Turkish Embassador at Rome, who took a kindly interest in our enterprise, obtained for us the seven curious samples, exhibited in No. XL, in the cases and told us that the Turkish word used for this lace is the term that is also applied to fuschias, hare-bells and other hanging flowers, as well as to dangling ornaments and earrings in Turkey.

No. XLI A and B cases are other pieces of Turkish lace which belong to Lady Layard, the material in which they are manufactured is white silk and they were made according to the old Turkish system in the embroidery schools founded under her ladyship's auspices in Constantinople. In these laces the garlands and sprays of flowers are made to interlace while preserving the bell-like characteristics of the antique laces from which their **designs** have been adapted to modern taste. Turkish ladies at present, dress like their European sisters and the real and imitation lace they wear is all sent with their toilettes from Paris; but these veils and scarfs which have resisted innovations of French fashion, are still trimmed with narrow Turkish edgings. The Constantinople school of embroidery has revived many old oriental stitches and designs, and tends to keep up the artistic traditions of Turkish needle work and its influence is greatly appreciated by English visitors and tradesmen, and a ready sale is found for its products.

After considering with so much care all these early efforts towards the production of needle lace, for evidently the Turkish silk laces are made according to the Jewish traditions which had their origin in Egypt, the following deductions seem the most plausible, namely: That on emerging from the barbarity attendant on the decline and fall of the Western Empire, the people of Europe began to realize the attraction of riches obtained by peaceful barter or sales, instead of snatched with rude violence from weaker neighbors, to be shortly again lost by the same lawless means they, in their turn, meeting a stronger opponent. The desire of artistically adorning their persons, their homes and above all their churches 'which were no longer threatened with perpetually recurring pillage and destruction, quickly followed the realization of stable fortune. Hidden away behind thick walls from the din and clatter of arms raised by the boisterous race which had poured out from the north and over- run the Roman possessions, the sister arts of embroidery and lace-making practised by the cunning daughters of the needle were still to be found in the dwellings of the Jewish and oriental merchants who had settled on every part of the Mediterranean coast. Rich and rare mediæval silk laces unrivalled even by the most celebrated specimens preserved in the Christian churches and cathedrals are still to be found in the old Italian synagogues. The energy that predominates in the European character belonged alike to Jewish teachers and to their Christian pupils and caused them to exercise their vivid imaginations in the development of these arts until products of rarest beauty were created upon our continent, whereas the embroiderers of Oriental race who have

ever been governed by an almost rabid conservatism have remained without developing for centuries, thus preserving for us
the old traditions even as far back as the type of needle work
that was used on Aaron's ephod three thousand years ago. All
the silk passementerie and the gold, silver and polychrome laces
of the earliest renaissance in Italy were made by the Jews, who
were also the chief producers of other varieties of lace in Spain
where this purple was richer than in Italy and exhibited much
greater luxury in the appointment of its places of worship as well
as in its homes than did the semi-barbarous Christians. When
the Jews were reduced to penury by perpetual persecutions and
confiscations which ended in their expulsion from Spain, they
made use of these arts to maintain themselves in the places
whither they fled and as there was a constantly increasing demand
for trimmings and laces all over Southern Europe they were able
with thrift to form small factories in which they employed
apprentices who soon became skilled workwomen and helped
them to execute the numerous orders they received. These
pupils became teachers in their turn and spread the knowledge
of and taste for laces and gimps so that when later another wave
of persecution came (this time turned against the protestants)
a great many of those who belonged to that faith had learned
lace-making as a pleasant pastime, and so fleeing to protestant
England, Germany and Sweden, carried the art farther afield
becoming diligent bread-winners and intelligent teachers in their
turn. But another cause was also at work in the middle ages
long before the protestant persecutions which caused the Christians to eagerly study lace-making so as not to require Jewish
assistance in the production of lace.

Perhaps, like many ceremonies in the Christian Church the
custom of using fringes and laces on the vestments of the priest
and on church linen was copied from the Jewish ritual, but when
intolerance and cruelty toward the Hebrew race prevailed, the
Christian women sought to learn all of the secrets of lace
making and then develop new varieties of lace; their piety spur-
ring them to intense activity by horror at the thought of decking
the altar consecrated to the Holy Trinity with the work of un-

believers. The art once implanted among the pious women rapidly became a source of amusement and rivalry in the narrow lives of the nuns and cloistered ladies, who dedicated all their energies deprived of natural outlets, to the invention of new stitches and more wonderful traceries, both in lace and embroideries, until the superb Venetian point laces and needle paintings sprung into existence under their magic touch. These reflections inspired by art needle-work and lace are also applicable to bobbin lace, but whence came it? How was it invented or evolved out of weaving? A blue *lace* bound the diadem upon the brow of the Jewish High Priest; this lace cannot have been simply a cord, but a flat fabric—for tradition says it was wrought in colors and fringed at the ends, resembling a passamenterie, gimp or macrame lace—but the question remains unanswered as to whether it was worked with bobbins; and writers about lace have filled pages with speculation on this subject and quoted from Moses and the Prophets, always ending, however, with the assertion that the first positive evidence of the existence of bobbin lace is an Italian document of the fifteenth century, of which we will later on produce a part, or a Dutch woodcut of the sixteenth century, whilst all the time the sands of Egypt and rich soil of Italy have been reserving their incontrovertible evidence.

The Phrygians, Assyrians, Persians and other inhabitants of Southwestern Asia, like the Tartars of today, all wore conical caps and introduced the use of this headgear into the countries to which they emigrated, o. with which they traded. To the Phrygians, who very early over-ran northern Greece, is due the use in that country of woolen caps during the winter, and of flaxen nets shaped as conical fillets, during the warm months.

, Caps became the fashion in Egypt with the introduction of the religion of Mythras by the Persians, the priests of that religion retaining them even while officiating and they were everywhere considered a sign of freedom and no slaves were allowed to wear them; for the ceremony used in liberating a slave consisted precisely in the placing of a red cap on his head and acclaiming him as an equal. This cap was sometimes used of an etruncated shape like the fez and in this form it must have given

5

origin to that Mahometan head covering just as in the original pointed shape it became the model for the Doge's *corno* or crown and the Liberty caps placed on the heads of Brittania and her fair daughter—Columbia, although the original color was abandoned.

In the days of the French craze for classicism, the Republicans re-dyed this emblem of liberty in the blood of aristocrats and waving it aloft as their standard acclaimed it with its original name of " Phrygian Cap." Caps of this shape must have become universally the fashion at the time when the Persian religion of Mythras gained ascendancy among civilized nations, which was just before the Christian era and its communistic tenets resisted the Christian religion in Rome even after the general conversion of the Latins and had so strongly impressed the popular mind that some of its forms have survived in the present rites of Free Masonry.

No. XLII screen, is a drawing taken from a bas relief in the Louvre museum and represents these caps as worn by the priests of Mythras. We may judge from the number of fragments of them found in the graves in Panapolis, that they were universal in use.

No. XLV screen, is a section of an etruncated woolen cap; the little sketches, A, B, C, D, show the way in which it was worn, and that its shape must have greatly resembled that of the knitted and crocheted ones worn by our own young people. The winter caps were made of red wool, or were striped in colors, with a card in the edge to tighten them to the head if necessary.

No. XLVI A screen and No. XLVII A screen are also pieces of the same kind of caps while No. XLVI B and No. XLVII B are new pieces that were copied from them by the young lace makers in the school at Brazza, No. XLVII C is a photograph of some fragments numbered 12, 15, 16, of the same kind of work. These caps are neither knitted nor crocheted, for the meshes do not consist of loops, neither are they embroidered, for the threads are continuous and we find no knots. All the learned professors, who have seen them, unite in saying they were interlaced by the fingers, but how they cannot tell, as they have found no lace bobbins in connection with them; still they *are* made with bobbins, for without a reel at the end of the threads to shorten them to the desired length by winding them around something while working it would be quite impossible to avoid most hopeless tangles and whole series of gordian knots. Allowing for the difference in wool and the regularity produced by constantly working the same design, the copies made by the inexperienced Italian children in the lace school are not bad; the girls worked by interlacing two bobbins instead of the four that are at present used in in the manufacture of lace and they were forced to twirl the bobbins from left to right, which is the exact contrary of the twist now given and very aggravating when one is accustomed to modern work.

No. XLVII B, C, D, screen show the manner of weaving these caps in ancient times as well as the linen thread nets in summer, and also represents a Neapolitan fisherman with one of these same caps which are still worn by men of his class along the coasts of Italy, Spain and France.

No. XLVIII screen is a perfectly preserved quarter of one of the thread nets, bound with red wool.

No. XLIX screen is a quarter of a lace net, executed in a different design.

No. L screen is a well preserved and fresh looking half net of more elaborate lace, executed with remarkable precision.

No. LI case is unique of its kind, being a complete lace net or bonnet made of soft thread with red binding, which has been placed on a barber's pole, to show with what a graceful effect these nets were worn. Beside it there is placed No. LII, giving an idea of a classic lace cushion with the same kind of lace net mounted on it in process of execution by means of wooden bobbins copied from the bone ones of that epoch for *miribile dictu*. Last spring (1892), while we were in Rome planning our exhibit, Prof. E. Brizio, director of the Etruscan Museum, in Bologna, was excavating among the ruins of the old Roman town of Claterna, ten miles from Bologna, on the Emilian Way, and

St. Ambrose describes it as already classified among the ruinous cities in A. D. 393.

Here, at the bottom of a filled-up well of Roman construction, the professor found a quantity of little, solid, long wasp-shaped cylinders, the use of which he could not understand, as they resembled none of the Roman implements with which he was acquainted, nor any object in use in modern times ; and this is natural, considering he is a professor of quite another matter than lace-making, and that he moreover lives in a part of the world where lace is not at present produced.　Soon, however, the mystery was solved for him, as in passing a bric-a-brac dealer his eye was attracted by a lace-maker's pillow with all its equipments on exhibition in the window.　He at once recognized that the bobbins hanging from this pillow were the counterparts of his curious bone cylinders, which clearly proved to his mind that he had here found the solution of the enigma not only of the bobbins from Claterna, but also of a similar instrument which had been for years in possession of the museum at Bologna.

Another proof which of course neither he nor anyone, who had not been accustomed to the manufacture of lace could imagine, lies in the fact that the bobbins were found in couples, or in groups formed of couples, with the exception of one little heap reduced to fragments, out of which he composed seven imperfect bobbins, beside a few small bits almost reduced to powder.　He has kindly furnished us with fac similes of these valuable proofs in the history of lace-making which are exhibited in the cases under Nos. LIII and LIV.

No. LIV (a) cases is a double-hooked crochet needle which has formed part of the collection existing in the museum at Bologna for many years, and no one knows its origin, although it is supposed to be Greek.

Cavaliere Augusto Castellani has in his superb gallery, which is full of Etruscan and Roman antiquities, a great many of these bobbins, but they were purchased among numbers of other Roman relics and in the old-fashioned way without inquiry as to the details attending their discovery; they, therefore, attracted no particular attention; indeed, owing to their shape, they were thought to be a kind of stylus for writing on wax, with a round head or classic rubber at the opposite end for canceling errors. The cavaliere, however, seemed quite converted when he observed that the knobs were often decidedly jagged or sharp whereas the end which should have been pointed (if a stylus) was usually as blunt, if not blunter, than the knob. During the seventeenth century, in the Hartz mountains and on the coasts of the North sea, the pioneers of pillow lace found the semi-barbarous peasant and fisher-women making elastic caps and nets for the men's heads by plaiting threads together with rude bone bobbins used by twos instead of by fours, following the same process which the modern lace girls were forced to adopt in imitating the Panopolis lace nets. History adds that these women learned with surprising rapidity the art of complicated lace making, and became, in a short time, proficient and artistic lace makers. Neapolitan fishermen and Spanish mule drivers of to-day, both "on and off the stage," cover their curly locks with pointed nets made in red silk or wool, and in the time of the troubadours, gallants and pages alike still wore them as we see depicted in portraits and historical paintings. In England the old lace makers in Devonshire still call their bobbins "bones," because they say formerly they were made of small pieces of sheep's bones and, that owing to this, they call their bobbin lace "bone lace."

The early annals of England and other countries mention teaching new stitches and designs, and contain notes on the importation of clever teachers from other parts to instruct the natives in new stitches and fresh designs, but not with the object of founding a new industry. We may thus consider pillow-lace to be a direct inheritance from classic times; an inheritance, which, though possessed of rich possibilities, long lay fallow till in the fifteenth and sixteenth centuries it was found of easy cultivation and productive of most gorgeous blossoms.

Perhaps longer and closer study than was possible during the few months at our command in which to prepare this exhibit would bring to light more facts about the origin of this art and search still further into the remote past. After the long journeys which we have been forced to take for a field in search of the earliest

proofs of the manufacture of lace, we will enter the fair garden in which the splendid flowers and luxuriant grasses of nature
have been transformed by the magic of gentle fingers into beautiful, curious and everlasting hybrids, formed of that European
kingdom in which the ideal and material are continually at war
and yet ever exert an artistically happy reaction upon each
other, and once in Italy we will not again leave that sunny land,
for busy merchants will bring to its markets the produce of other
countries and will recount narratives of what they saw on their
travels. But before crossing the threshold of the Middle Ages,
we must take one more peep below the soil and see what remains
of the costumes of the Umbrians and the Etruscans of the civilized inhabitants of Italy when the land was young.

No. LV screen represents an Umbrian cinerary urn of the eighth
century B. C. These urns were always covered with a veil or
cloth and the rude drawings that decorate them usually represent
a net with dentated edges trimmed with tassels and much resembling the nets used in the well-known Gitana or Spanish Gipsy
costume.

No. LVI screen is the design of an archaic, Greek figure with
borders painted on the garments to represent colored embroidery.
Some writers on lace speak of such borders as evidences of the
use of bobbin lace at that period, but it strikes us that this forms
but a weak foundation on which to build any serious argument.

No. LVIII screen is a figure of Minerva copied from the painting on one of the Parthenopean vases of about the fourth
century, B. C.

No. XXXVIII screen is a charmingly graceful figure of the same
Goddess, beautifully drawn, and is copied from an exquisite vase
in the Estruscan Museum in Rome; it most decidedly appears to
reproduce a kind of open work or lace indicated as adorning the
edge of her lighter garments.

Beside this figure on the same card there is a drawing natural
size, of a bifurcated netting needle exactly like those which are
found in great numbers in the Tiber, and judging from its small-
ness it must have served for the manufacture of fine hair-nets.

No. LVIII screen represents a golden bracelet or cuff of the sixth or seventh century B. C. The original of this bracelet was evidently copied from needle work consisting of drawn work alternated with bands of linen; it was found in the Vetulonia excavations made in 1890, and belongs to the Etruscan Museum in Florence. Professor Milani, Director of that institute, which is the first of its kind in Italy, tells me that there exist ample proofs of the use of delicate embroidery, open work, net and woven fringes for the embellishment of the toilet by Greeks and Etruscans, but he feels persuaded that bonafide pillow lace made with bobbins was unknown to these peoples.

While talking with him, I observed in his studio a Greek platter dating from the end of the fifth century B. C.; it was made of rare white "*patrina*," and on it was depicted the nymph *Arachne*, who dared to compete with Minerva in the arts of the loom and the needle. The subjects of the designs she composed were more earthly than were those of the austere goddess, and we see her here, seated in pensive attitude while Eros whispers advice into her ear and one of his companions traces a scroll on the web placed before her which is designed with all the graceful curves that characterize Venetian point.

Minerva transformed her unhappy rival into a spider, thus condemning her forever to weave those magic circles and cobwebs with which vies the work of human fingers in the making of lace. This Greek legend may be based on some fact adorned by the romantic imagination of a bygone poet, or it may have originated in metaphor alone, in any case to its inspiration are due the charming odes of the Renaissance in which the poets perpetually attribute the creation of the arts of embroidery to the needle of Minerva, while the invention of the subtler and more delicate art of lace making is ascribed to Arachne. These poets, in their verses entwined the ancient Greek fable with the arts and designations of lace stitches known to them producing a quaint effect—even as the fair fingers, whose praises they sang, so deftly interlaced the threads of silk and gold.

Thus Agnolo Firenzuolo who wrote about 1520, in his "Elegia sopra un Collaretto" describes with loving lingering detail a piece of lace that caught his fancy.

Questa collar scolpe la donna mia
This collar was sculptured by my lady.
Di basso rilevar ch' Arachne mai
In bas-reliefs such as Arachne.
E chi la vinse non faria piu bello.
And she who conquered her ne'er could excel.
Mira quel bel fogliame ch' un acanto.
Look on that lovely foliage like an Acanthus
Sembra che sopra un mur'vada carponi
Which o'er a wall its branches trails.
Mira quei fior 'ch 'un candido ne cade.
Look on these pure white flowers.
Vicino al seme apre la boccia l' altro.
Which near the open pods hang in harmony.
Quel cordiglin ch 'l legan d'ognintorno.
That little cord that binds each one about.
Come si levan ben! Mostrando ch 'ella.
How it stands out, proving that she who wrought.
E' la vera maestra di quest' arte.
Is very mistress of this art.
Come ben compartitison guei punti!
How well distributed are all those points!
Ve come son equal quei bottoncelli.
See the equality of all those little knobs.
Come s'alzano in guisa d'un bel colle.
Which rise as fair as beauteous hills.
L'un come l'altro
One like the other.
Questi merli di man questi trafori.
This hand made lace ; this open work.
Fece pur 'ella e questa punta a spina.
Is all produced by her, this herring bone.
Che mette in mezzo questo cordoncello.
Which in the midst holds down a little cord.
Ella li fe pure, ella lo fece.
Is also made by her; all wrought by her.
No. LXVII cases and the following numbers are specimens of

the various implements used in spinning, knitting, embroidery and lace-making throughout the ages.

No. LVII is a distaff used for spinning flax and was made by a peasant of Moruzzo, the township in the province of Friuli, in which the Castello di Brazza is situated. This distaff ends in a colored ball and is beautifully and artistically carved, the inspiration of the original design having come from the heart of the carver who made it as a gift to his affianced. On it he has represented their persons, their homes and their hearts, four-leaved clovers, horse-shoes, and an infinity of other emblems of love and fortune. Hanging from it is the spindle and it is attached to the wall by the wrought brass pins by which the peasant women support the distaff, utilizing their belts as rests while spinning as they walk along the roads or following the sheep across the pasture.

No. LXVI wall was carved by the same man later in life, as a gift to his daughter; the hearts are therefore represented as having flowered truly a very pretty and poetic conceit, for an uneducated peasant. The end of this distaff consists of a two-pronged brass fork resembling a trident which is used in spinning wool.

These two simple implements, rendered so artistic by an untutored hand inspired by love, form a true illustration of the affectionate nature and devotion to the beautiful that characterize the Italian people in general, so that lace making and straw plating which require taste as well as skill, come naturally to every daughter of the people.

No. LVIII 1, 2, 3, 4, 5, 7, 8, 9 cases are specimens of the spindle whirls used in spinning by hand in different parts of the world. They date from the period of stone age and the lake dwellers down to the present day.

In Europe the spinning wheel was early invented, but in certain parts of Italy the women still prefer the old fashioned distaff which enables them to spin at odd times when it would be impossible to use a wheel.

No. LVIII (*b*) cases is a complete ivory spindle of classic times and was found in Greece. Such specimens as this are extremely rare.

No. LVIII 10 cases is the only wooden spindle with earthenware whirl attached which has been as yet discovered. It was found at Achmin, Panapolis, and might have served to spin the flax out of which some of our specimens of stuffs were woven.

No. LX cases are twenty-three Peruvian specimens, and date from a time long anterior to the discovery of America by Christopher Columbus. They are also especially interesting in connection with our subject as the mummies with which they were found were clothed in the same kind of textiles as those found at Achmin, thus showing that a kindred civilization existed at an early date in the old and new world, the evidence afforded by the one necropolis completing and corroborating that of the other.

We have here also spindles and knitting and other needles with the yarn still on them, covered by small cases to protect their points, as also an ordinary ball of blue cotton that might have come from the work basket of a modern housewife.

No. LX (*b*) cases is a fac-simile of the already mentioned double-hooked crochet needle which is preserved in the Etruscan Museum in Bologna.

No. LXI (*a, b, c*) cases is a sketch made by Herr R. Torrer, of very rare prehistoric needles, which it was impossible to borrow, or have duplicated in time for the Exhibition. It will be noticed that A and B (natural sizes) which were taken from the homes of of the cave dwellers of Thayngen, are more perfect in form than is D, a bone needle (also natural size) of the stone age from the lake dwellings at Bauchanze on Lake Zurich. The cave dwellers were in many things more civilized than were their successors, the lake dwellers, and must have embroidered on leather with quills and grasses, and dressed and lived as do their prototypes, the Esquimaux and the Alaskan Indians today.

No. LXI D cases is a drawing of a wooden hook which is now in the Swiss National Museum at Zurich. It has a disc to facilitate the boring of holes in skins or textiles, while the hook served to draw through the thread or grass destined to form a fringe or embroidery.

No. LXII cases consists of nine antique needles. Nos. 1, 2, 3, 4 are examples of the early " bores" called " *prieme*," the use of which preceded that of needles as shaped and used by us. No. 2 is made of rudely carved bone, and dates from the lake dwellings of the Stone Age; 3 and 4 are of bronze and are from lake dwellings of the Bronze Age; while 5 is a *knobbed prieme*, or eyeless needle of horn from the lake dwellings of the Stone Age. In using this kind of implement a hole was bored with the point and then it served to draw through the thread tied to its knobbed head. No. 6 is the same kind of instrument from the Lake Dwellings of the Bronze Age. No. 7 is a coarse, round eyed needle of the Bronze Age, from Italy. No. 8 is a fine long eyed needle of the Bronze Age from the lake dwellings of the Groserzafen on Lake Zurich.

No. LXIII cases is a drawing of a most elegantly designed needle stuck through a coil of gold thread. It was found in a tomb at Vesentium, and is now the property of the Etruscan Museum in Florence.

Under No. LXL are exhibited six fac similes of the Roman bone bobbins found last May, 1892, by Professor Brizio at Claterna, which we have already mentioned, and which are now lying with the others found at the same time in the Bologna museum, while the seventh and smallest bobbin is the one which previously existed in the rich Roman collection at the museum and its origin is unknown. Finally we exhibit four wooden bobbins, such as are used in the great centers of Italian lace making, namely, Venice, Genoa and Cantu (near Milan,) and one of the covered kind used in Saxony, which has been adopted in Friuli, because it keeps the thread cleaner. In closing this division of our book which refers exclusively to the production of woman's agile fingers when the art of needle and bobbin lace making was in its infancy, we present a little ragged child's sock of great rarity and value though apparent worthlessness. No. LXVIII cases is the earliest known example of knitting and the only socks as yet found in the excavations of Achmin's Panopolis. It is ribbed and striped in red, purple and black, the knitting being executed with great neatness and loving care, so as to assure the comfort and protection of the little foot it was

destined to cover from the chilling blasts of winter, and it·is so
well preserved that one might doubt its authenticity did not the
divided toes and seamless heal—the instep being seamed instead
—prove it to have been made to wear with a Roman sandal, of
which the strap fitted the holes (existing between the toes and
on the instep) one thousand five hundred years ago!

As we look on this most ancient baby sock, this little relic so
long preserved in the vast ocean of Egyptian sands, to be at last
cast up for our instruction and to show us that the world, in
many things, has not changed so much as we often imagine and
we are led to realize, that mothers spun and knitted to keep their
children warm, and that little ones ran and jumped and wore out
clothes and patience then, just as they do now. These thoughts
cause a great tenderness to swell up in the feminine heart toward
the long past generation, and the dry bones and dust are again
clothed with life. Plainly we see before us the little Christian
lads of Panopolis clattering through the great gates, and off to
school with sandaled feet and their agile bodies clothed with
tunics and warm togas trimmed with pretty designs illustrative
of thoughts pleasing to children, while their heads are covered
with the long bright woolen caps, such as we have exhibited, and
each boy, with strapped slate and tablet slung across a shoulder,
gives himself an· air of importance and manliness, though his
young mind is much more intent on fun and frolic, and tricks
innumerable, than on the difficult passages in the history of
Julius Cæsar, his Latin grammar or his Greek translation.

PART III.

The Renaissance.

The word *renaissance* (literally re-birth) is accepted as the definition of the awakening of the European mind to beauties in nature, art and literature, from the profound sleep and troubled dreams of superstition, interrupted by the long nightmares of barbarian and Gothic invasions which followed upon the fearful orgies in which the Roman empire expired.

The Christian church in its teaching and decorations preserved a tradition of the past, but the heavenly flame of art was so buried beneath the ashes of strife, controversy and narrow-mindedness, that the feeble spark which perpetuated its eternal fire was unrecognizable.

In Byzantium alone it flickered up a little amid the gorgeous costumes and decorations of church and court which warmed the imagination, and here as in Sicily—which, owing to its insular form and its southern position, suffered less acutely from invasions—we find that the gentle art of lace-making continued.

When the Saracens conquered Northern Africa, Sicily and Spain, they caused the inhabitants to instruct them, as well as to assist them in producing and perfecting articles for which they were already celebrated.

No. 70, from A to Y inclusive, on the screen, consists of a few precious rags found in an Hyspano-moresque tomb of the eleventh or twelfth century. They fill the void between the lace caps of Achmin-panopolis and the first examples of Venetian work, and they give us the earliest piece of point lace made entirely with a needle and thread without other material used as a foundation. These samples are in a much worse state of preservation and are much more fragile than those from Achmin, being appar-

ently records of a more remote date, but this condition is produced by the difference of climate.

No. 70 *a*, screen, is a piece of lace knotted as in *Punto in Aria*
and made entirely with the needle out of linen thread, well
waxed so as to stiffen it, and wound with gold foil; it formed a
part of a helmet-shaped head dress.

No. 70 *b*, screen, is a piece of red ribbon used to cover the
seams which united the four quarters of the above-mentioned
head dress, and is braided in fine gold and silver thread spun
with linen or cotton, as is done in the East to-day.   The design
of the braiding is roughly sketched on the card board by the
side of the ribbon, as is also that of the broader ribbon, 70 *c*, used
to edge the head dress.

No. 70 *e*, screen, is a piece of the finest gauze veiling woven
of silk or flax.   It was evidently used under the head dress and
allowed to float loose over the hair and shoulders so as to be
drawn across the face when desired.

No. 70 *f*, screen, is a piece of the border of such a veil wrought
in silver with groups of tiny silver tassels at regular intervals,
which must have had a charming effect in the sunlight when all
was new, white and dazzling.

No. 70 *h*, screen, is a piece of thin material striped in silver and
gold, such as we call *bayadere* stuff, and may be a piece of the
skirt or shawl which formed part of this costume.

No. 70 *j* is a piece of the same kind of material, bordered
with a very fine fringe, and evidently is part of a scarf or sash.

No. 70 *i* is a piece of fine thin cloth of gold.

No. 70 *g* is a piece of real bobbin lace, composed of aloes
fibre instead of flax, such as was made everywhere in the islands
and on the northern coast of the Mediterranean for centuries,
and it shows a great advance in workmanship from the lace of
Achmin-Panopolis, for here the bobbins are used in pairs instead of single, that is to say four are interwoven instead of two,
and the threads are therefore combined in the same way as every
lace-maker twirls them to-day.

In the little sketch No. 70 II we have the whole head-dress reconstructed in its bright original colors and the mind at once reverts

to the Crusades and Richard Coeur de Lion, Saladin and the fair women made so popular by Sir Walter Scott in his novel of Ivanhoe; and as we continue to gaze, these heroes and heroines of a bygone age become materialized and move and breathe in actual reality, called into life by these old Moorish rags, causing us to realize that with all the riches and barbaric splendor, move-ment and strife of this epoch, the art of lace making continued to develop.

Under the last of the western emperors, the Goths and the Byzantines, Rome was abandoned as the capital and seat of gov-ernment in Italy transferred to the more easily fortified seaport of Ravenna. In the mosaics that adorn this city's unique basil-icas, which were constructed in the sixth century, are found the only perfect remains of Italian art of that period, and jt will be seen from the *photographs exhibited by Countess Passolini with the lace from her school at Coccalia*, that the Empress Theodora and the ladies who formed her court wore costumes composed of the same stuff as the fragments from Achmin; one of the ladies in particular carries over her arm a worked, fringed veil resembling those still in use in Turkey, which is interesting in illustrating our special branch of textile art.

No. 71 screen is a narrow piece of blue bobbin lace of which three examples only are known to exist in Italy. It was sent in the eleventh century from Constantinople to Spezia, then known as *Lemi*. The blue square mesh ground is made entirely by bobbins, and is the same as that of all old Italian and Sicilian lace, in aspect resem-bling a very fine net. It is embroidered with little white birds, made in the same darning stitch as was used in the Gobelin style of embroidery found at Achmin. This kind of lace must have been the *Lacinia* of the Latins, from which the English term *lace* is derived, and was in general use in the twelfth and thir-teenth centuries. References are constantly found in old books to blue "*borders*" or "*friezes*" embroidered in white birds and lions which evidently was this kind of work.

No. 72 cases is an altar cloth trimmed with a variety of this blue lace embroidered in white, exhibited, as well as many of the following examples, by Mrs. Arthur Bronson, of Venice. In it

the design is of the fifteenth century and the bobbin ground
(called *maglia quadra*), and the embroidery is much more roughly
executed than in No. 71. It has a pretty blue and white antique pillow lace called "*campane*" sewed on the edge. The mixing of two
or more colors was very fashionable, as were also all the *polychrome* or divers colored laces in the fifteenth century. The perfection of the campane, or edging, and the negligence in the execution of the Byzantine lace in No. 71 prove the change of style
which had occurred before its manufacture, for in the fifteenth
century this lace which could but produce a stiff effect rapidly
lost ground before the newer and more varied and graceful trimmings, composed of embroidered net, and of "*punto a groppo*," now
called Macrame and complicated bobbin laces. The following are
also examples of Byzantine lace, or "*maglia quadra*," and show
what rich effect could be produced in this simple kind of work
with symmetrical designs and happy blending of materials and
colors.

No. 500 cases is made with a blue silk ground, embroidered
in buff silk and white thread; it belongs to S‌i nora Antoinette
Costa of Rome, as does No. 488 cases, which is a piece made all
in white linen thread, and destined for use on the end of a towel.

No. 86 cases is the same kind of lace, but produces a very
different effect, the ground being made in thread of aloes dyed
brown, and embroidered in "*punto a scacchetti*," or square point with
an unconventional pattern executed in silks exquisitely tinted in
brown, heliotrope, green and yellow.

No. 78 cases belongs to Mrs. Bronson. The ground is made
with soft floss-like ecru thread and embroidered with "*punto a
spina*," or "thorn stitch," in delicate buff yellow and peacock blue
and green silk. Along the edge runs a most interesting and rare
antique polychrome, "campane" lace of fine silk. This repeats
the colors and the design of the wider lace, and was evidently
made on purpose to edge it.

No. 339 screen is an interesting sample of the same, dating
from the twelfth or thirteenth century, to judge from the design
and is embroidered in red and green silk.

No. 341 screen is embroidered in cream and blue silk and dates from the fourteenth century.

No. 347 screen is embroidered in red silk and belongs to the same period.

The designs in Nos. 355 and 357 screens indicate work of the early part of the sixteenth century.

A modified Byzantine lace was also made entirely with bobbins and fine white thread. It consisted of narrow bands of a close ground, ornamented by the simple geometrical designs or stiff conventional flowers, outlined in open work, small as pin holes.

The sample No. 95 screen and the frill in the pink and silver brocaded baby cap No. 130 (of the sixteenth century) are of this lace; it was used throughout Europe to trim baby clothes, and is still to be found on antique baptismal garments, (such as for example the brocaded cap) which have been religiously preserved in certain old families on the continent and in England from generation to generation.

Mrs. Bury Palliser in her celebrated book on lace speaks of this baptismal lace as well as of blue wedding lace which was made at Coventry in England, during the middle ages, and which it was the custom to distribute to all members of the bridal party. She quotes an account of Queen Elizabeth's visit to Kenilworth, in which the youths of that parish are described as walking in front of the procession carrying branches of fresh broom and wearing *"blue bridal lace* as if they were groomsmen at a wedding." With the spread of puritanism and of the harsh decrees it inspired, the old custom, like many others, died out in England, as did also the manufacture of the celebrated blue thread in Coventry. Mrs. Palliser adds that no relics of this lace now remain in England, but it must have resembled the above examples. In this case as in many others, we find proofs of the much earlier Renaissance of the arts in Italy than in England, embroidery alone excepted, this is explained by the fact that a powerful unbroken tradition remained in the English convents of the artistic needle-work learned from the Phrygians, so that the *"opus phrygianum"* of the ancients was merged in the celebrated and even more beautiful "opus Anglicanun. The

6

frigidity of the climate tended to keep the women at home and alive to the attractions of a sedentary occupation which they could follow beside the hearth, and it naturally caused them to prefer embroidery to lace; airy open work and transparent fabrics not being suited to their cold, sunless, stonebuilt homes, either for household or personal linen, until time and fashion introduced luxury in the household appointments, and collars, frills and cuffs as adornments to necks and sleeves, these becoming objects being purely accessories of the toilet, the volume and not the quality of which could affect physical comfort.

The first examples of lace and *punto tagliato* in England, such as the shroud of St Cuthbert, who was buried in Durham cathedral in the twelfth century, and his vestments which are preserved in the library of the chapter as well as the open work and lace reproduced on the earliest monuments, all belong to the ecclesiastics, and may have been brought from Italy as attributes of the church ritual in exchange for the English embroideries so much prized by the popes and cardinals in Rome. We find, however, that in 1863, under Edward IV, gold and silk lace trimmed the garments of the laity, for an edict which that monarch then promulgated forbade their use. They were all imported from Italy, and Richard III, at his coronation in 1438, wore a robe of crimson satin laced with two bands of gold and silk *passement*, which had been made in Venice on purpose for this occasion.

The Queen of the Adriatic, owing to her commercial intercourse with Byzantium and the Orient, was throughout the Middle Ages the most luxurious and refined city of Europe, and from a very early date in her existence minute descriptions of costumes with the prices paid for their component parts were noted in documents which have been carefully preserved in her state archives. Thus, in 1219, we learn from an old account book that tailors charged twice as much for a border of needle-work, called "*fregio*," or "*frixatura*," as they did for one of fine fur, which indicates that the work must have been very elaborate. Frequent allusions to various kinds of trimmings are found in the registers kept, during the fourteenth century, by the Venetian customs officers as well as in the account books and records of lawsuits, divisions and wills belonging to private families. In the earliest mosaics of the church of St. Mark these trimmings are also rudely represented alike on the garments of grotesque saints and disfigured mortals; they are also reproduced with minute faithfulness of detail in the more gracefully executed miniatures which enrich the manuscripts of that period.

No. 89 screen is taken from a manuscript of the thirteenth century, which contains the statutes and by-laws of the guild of Bologna bakers; it represents an angel presenting St. Mary Magdalen, who is depicted as kneeling in her hermitage, with a scarf or toga edged with a blue lace border and fringe.

No. 113 screen consists of four sketches taken from the illuminated headings of the "*Rotuli*," or rolls of the University, which are preserved in the Archives of Bologna, those chosen for reproduction being dated from 1439 to 1455. In them the bishop, Petronius, the martyr, and (Patron Saint of Bologna), is represented in full canonicals with his right hand raised in the act of blessing the University, whilst in his left he holds the walled city, recognizable, owing to the exaggerated representation of the Towers of the Garisenda and of the Asinelli. His mantle is edged with fur, and the broad trimming on his glove and sleeve illustrates the lace of the period, namely *Reticella*, which must have just come into fashion and have deeply impressed the limner, for in the earlier and later Rotuli, though the execution of the painting is more artistic and the designs are more beautiful and floreate, we do not find the lace on the vestments distinctly reproduced. These Rotuli are written on parchment superbly illuminated, and form an almost complete series from 1438 to 1799, besides a few scattered numbers of the fourteenth century. They have never been published, although they constitute an exhaustive and unequalled illustration of miniature painting in Italy. These rolls contain the list of the *persons* (for celebrated women as well as men figure among the lecturers) who were called by the Rectors, with the approbation of the civic authorities, to read or teach on various subjects, which with the hours allotted to each are minutely described and enumerated; two rolls were issued **every** year, one for the " Jurists " and one for the " Artists."

In 1347 people still called gowns, *tunics*, and several for women and children are described as *"laboratum ad intayos,"* *i. e.*, worked with open or carved work from which the term *punto tagliato* originated. Other tunics are mentioned as trimmed with an exaggerated quantity of gold, silver, pearl or glass buttons, and richly wrought button-holes. The sleeves were the most elaborate part of these costumes and reached to an enormous size, vying with the fashion of to-day; they were loaded with buttons and loops innumerable, and profusely trimmed with gold and beaded *"tressas,"* or tressed work, which can have been no other than a kind of gimp or passement as its name indicates. One tunic in particular is described as having a "low-cut" body," the first I find noted, and the usual rich sleeves; *trains*, or trailing skirts, are also mentioned as forming part of the women's costumes of this period. Until the end of the fourteenth century these superfluous buttons, jeweled borders and fur linings continued to be the fashion despite the constant edicts published against the abuse of ornament and the extravagance of the toilets, such as the one of 1299 limiting the price of borders to *5 Lire di piccoli per ell;* it must have been their costliness and uncomfortable weight, combined with the fear of prosecution that caused gold, silver and clinquant (plated metal), passements, laces and open-work insertions to replace them. The demand for every kind of trimming at this period was so great that their manufacturers became rich and powerful, so that in 1343 they were allowed to detach themselves from the association of weavers of which, until then, they had formed part, and organize in a separate guild formed of the producers of gold, silver, linen and silk thread, cords, lacings, gimps, fringes, "doppione," and all other articles used as or in the production of trimmings. They received the title of Master's *"Bordorum subtilum de filo subtili,"* which denomination must have been chosen as appropriate to lace-makers, for even after their craft became a great source of wealth and glory to Venice, this epithet, denominating the guild of which they formed part, remained unchanged.

The repeated edicts published by the Patriarchal and Protec-

tionist governments, forbidding the importation and limiting the
width and value of trimmings, forced the mercers to invent some
cheaper though effective edgings with which to supply their customers, and they naturally resorted to flax, aloes and silk as a
first material of comparatively small value in which to produce
pretty designs in drawn work, embroidered net, and above all,
bobbin lace, which being easy and rapid of execution, could be
sold with profit for a low price. These edgings, "frizidor,"
"smerli" or "merli" (so called from the Byzantine terms *mermis*,
bobbin and *mermiriso* to turn) were a novelty and pleasing to the
eye; besides, the customers found that they furnished the desired
trimmings for garments with the added charms of cheapness and
novelty, and so accepted them eagerly and they became the rage.
But as usual, once the fashion was established, rivalry in elegance
developed, and the original object was lost sight of; merchants
and consumers united in inciting the workwomen to fresh inventions, more perfect designs and minute details, until the beautiful
thread points of the golden age of lace became far more costly
and valuable than the jewelled borders which wrought such havoc
with the purses of the fourteenth century. In the surrounding
provinces the same conditions existed; in 1341 the Patriarch Ber-
trando of Aquileja, sovereign of the Patria (Friuli), forbade the
use of gold embroidery, but permitted a trimming of cord or lace
worth 40 francs per ell, a sum vastly superior in value to the
money used to-day, a price not to be surpassed under pain of
fines and excommunication. The will of the Countess Pierina
della Torre of Udine, dated 1396, mentions a silk kerchief ornamented with "merli," worked in gold leaves. These kerchiefs
for head and neck furnished a seductive field for the exhibition
of fine embroidery and lace. In a Venetian account book, under
various dates from 1437 to 1439, we find carefully registered a
great number of these articles of feminine adornment which are
perpetuated in the shawls, neckerchiefs and *Zeudade* or veils (see
No. 228 cases in tambour work of 1546) still worn by the Venetian patrician ladies on solemn occasions, and by the women of
the people daily. The kerchiefs were made of coarse *burato*,
linen, silk, muslin, or of the finest silk gauze brought from the

Orient and unrivalled by the products of modern industry. Those of the fifteenth century are described as *straforato*, literally excessively pierced with work in wheel shapes, such as we see in No. 407 and other samples on the screen and in No. 134 cases worked in "cartiglia," which belongs to Countess Valentinis of Friuli.

No. 126 cases is an heirloom in the historical Colleoni family. The kerchief dates from about 1600, and is made of the softest silk gauze, embroidered in very fine gold and silver thread with reversible open work and reliefs around the four sides. It was allotted the first prize assigned to this kind of work at the Historical Exhibition of Textile Arts, held in Rome in the spring of 1857.

No. 155 cases is evidently a neckerchief, being embroidered only on two sides of it, made of a sheer gauze, dating from the same period and embroidered very daintily and artistically with gold thread and gold foil, interspersed with conventional flowers and fruits exquisitely shaded in colored silks; owing to the daily use for which such objects were destined, specimens of them are very rare. The above mentioned Venetian account book also describes other kerchiefs worked with *chavi* (openings) in colored silks; this is a term used at that period for a simple variety of *punto tagliato* or *trapunto* (drawn work).

No. 93 screen is a fine specimen of this stitch having a design consisting of chimerical animals left in the linen with the reticulated open-work ground around them executed in red silk and edged with a narrow fringe worked in the material.

No. 335 screen has gold introduced in the ground and fringe.

No. 337 screen is very finely executed and dates from the thirteenth century; it is a most interesting sample of that curious work in human figures, animals and flowers left in linen, with an open-work ground, which was so much in vogue at the time of the troubadours.

No. 351 screen is purely gothic in design and is a sample of the open-work which, at that period, was imported into Italy from the Island of Rhodes.

No. 353 screen is of the fifteenth century and has a design of acorns and leaves worked in red silk.

Nos. 74 and 76 cases. These numbers represent two beautiful pieces of trapunto worked in *chavi* and equally finished on both sides. They belong to Mrs. Arthur Bronson. No. 74 forms the border for a bed-spread worked in a Byzantine design of mermaids, stags and dragons with little lions and small birds, interspersed among the principal figures to fill in the empty spaces. These creatures are left in the linen with the features worked by overcasting the design neatly in yellow silk, and the outlines are formed in the same way; the ground is embroidered in tiny openwork squares with the same silk, and the edge consists of a narrow silk fringe of the same color, wrought in the material which is characteristic of this kind of work.

No. 76 cases is made in very fine linen and must have served on a luxurious gown or apron. The design is of the renaissance, gracefully composed of large interlaced conventional foliage and scrolls; around this runs a beautiful simple border; the overcast outline and shading are everywhere composed of yellow silk and the fine reticulated ground is made in pale blue silk, the whole being edged with a narrow appropriate footing which has been subsequently added.

No. 324 cases is a pillow-case in fine white linen worked in trapunto with white thread with an all over gothic design.

No. 486 cases is an altar cloth or dresser scarf of the same kind of work belonging to Signora Costa and contains birds, animals and letters forming initials, monograms and words which stand out from the *cavato* ground owing to the superimposed embroidery and raised-work.

No. 492 cases belongs to the same proprietor and is unusually fine in material and work.

No. 605 cases comes from Ravenna; it is a table cloth in white linen worked in a Byzantine design and edged with antique pointed pillow lace of the fourteenth century.

No. 604 cases is a table cover of the same material and work but executed at a later date as is seen from the broad, beautiful Genoese pillow lace, composed of great wheels in oriental design,

most artistically executed which is sewed on either **end and in-**
dicates the beginning of the sixteenth century.

In the thirteenth and fourteenth centuries the colored embroideries called *punto crocettaa* as well as *trapunto* were very much appreciated, and in 1781, when the body of King Ferdinand the Second,
of Sicily, was discovered in a perfect state of preservation in the
royal sepulchres at Palermo, it was clothed in a shirt of the finest
linen with the collar and sleeves worked about in arabesques and
cufic inscription. This garment was made by the Saracens and
presented by their ruler to King Otto IV in 1210. At present
this species of work is again the fashion and as examples are rare
they are eagerly sought after by merchants and collectors and
command high prices. The "crocetta" embroidery is executed on
fine linen with bright colored silks in *scacchetti*, or square stitch, as
well as in back-chain-cross and other stitches, so neatly executed
that the finish of the wrong side is equal to that of the right; the
effect is generally enhanced by fringes wrought with the needle
into the edge of the border with the same tinted silks that compose the design.

Numbers 77 and 79 screen are samples of this work; the latter
is particularly fine in design and dates from the fifteenth century;
its chief interest lies in the well drawn and executed human
figures and animals of which it is composed, recalling the embroideries of the most artistic period of the Roman empire.

No. 632, 634, 636, 638 cases. These numbers represent twenty-
one superb examples of this kind of Italian embroidery, composing a rare collection brought together during years of research by Dr. Silvestrini, of Bologna, who has decided to sell
them. Supplemented by the *trapunto* and by embroideries from
Achmin-panopolis exhibited on the screen, these numbers afford
rare facilities for studying, at the source, the changes which in
the fifteenth century gradually stole over the art of designing for
decorative work, and the successful struggle made during the
renaissance to regain the lost congruities in composition. This
kind of embroidery continued the fashion until the seventeenth
century, and was used extensively on men's and women's body
linen alike, as is seen in portraits of this period, such as that of

the historical Count Hippolito di Porto in the museum at Vicenza, and as is recorded in all the court inventories and chronicles of Queen Elizabeth and her contemporaries.

Another Venetian document, dated 1439, is an inventory **of** the wardrobe belonging to Lorenzo Dona whilom, Governor of Friuli, and it repeats the same endless enumeration of fine cloth, silk, velvet and satin garments adorned with fur, goldlace, beads, metal, tinsel and silk gimps and borders under the names of *tarnato, frixo d'oro* and *d'oro Valenzane* (from Valencia, in Spain), *chamossa*, etc., while other documents mention *oro di Cologna* (from that city on the Rhine), *limbus phrygium, grammata, fimbria, tressas* and endless other terms all applied to the multitudinous trimmings of that day.

Other cities of Italy were not far behind Venice in the gaudiness of attire, for the constant intercourse with that great commercial centre, required by the exigiencies of trade furnished them with an opportunity for studying the fashions. Count Gaudini has spent years in forming the superb historical collection of textiles which bears his name in the museum of Modena; which is unsurpassed in this branch of art by any other in Europe, he has also patiently studied the masses of inedited documents relative to the ducal family of Este which reigned in Ferrara for so many centuries, and among their state archives, he has found mentioned in a register of the wardrobe, dated 1475 (a, c 25) a *frisco in oro di Cologna* (a frieze in gold of Cologne) and in that of 1476, dated June 5th, (a c 87) an order given for a felt hat "*Alla Borgognona,*" or in the Burgundian style, trimmed with a silver and silk gimp made with bobbins, "besides this (a c 96) in the same document is noted a seat made in velvet for the great hall," with the canopy trimmed at the sides with a trixetto (frill) in gold and silver made in little squares with bobbins; "finally in number 112, of the same collection are inscribed the orders for refurnishing an apartment in the palace, which had been given by the Duchess Eleonora, wife of Duke Hercules I, who desired these rooms to be embellished in honor of the expected visit to Ferrara of her sister, Beatrice of Aragon, on her journey to marry King Mathias Corvinus of Hungary In this manuscript one of the rooms is described as adorned with " a frieze of gold made with bobbins."

In Florence in the fifteenth century the luxury in clothes was quite equal to that of Venice, and Savonarola, in the stirring sermons which he preached,from 1484 to 1491 against the follies and extravagances of the time, frequently reproached the nuns, especially those of the convent of the Murate, with devoting their time to the vain fabrication of costly gold laces with which to adorn the houses and persons of the rich, instead of consecrating themselves to fasting, prayer and the glory of God in the embellishment of His holy temples.

No. 290 cases consists of a large quantity of this lace in perfect preservation, exhibited by Countess Agostini Venerosa della Seta, of Tuscany. It comprises the trimming for a table cover and contains the widest and best designs in gold lace I have ever seen. It comes from the fingers of those very women who provoked the great preacher's vituperation, and its glowing splendor corroborates his words.

After gazing on these jewels of textile art the eye turns with contempt from the seven samples (382) which are placed beside it, as also from Nos. 83 and 300, etc., on the screen which illustrate the gold, silver and clinquant laces made in other parts of Italy.

No. 85 screen is also Florentine bobbin lace of the same period as the gold lace. Its ground is made of unbleached thread, worked in the same way as the gold lace, but instead of the close designs shown in this it has two real *cartisane* (strips of parchment rolled with silk) interlaced with the ground in a conventional pattern to form the design. This kind of lace was called guipure, from *guiper* (in old French to roll), and its name after became synonymous with all lace made in a cord-like design.

No. 89 screen is an example of **an** entirely different kind of work, namely, of the first kind of net used in Italy as lace on garments. It is made of a very fine linen or silk mesh stiffened with wax and then embroidered in silk thread, and was the origin of lacis. It was in use during the fourteenth and early part of the fifteenth century, as is indicated by the design and proved by an account book formerly belonging to the Cathedral of Ferrara, and now existing in the municipal archives of that city. This document contains an entry made in 1469 of a bill presented by a certain Battista, wife of Nicolo Andrea, of Ferrara, for " repairing the very badly worn and damaged *gramito* (border) of fourteen surplices for the canons of the chapter, with detailed specifications of the work, together with the prices of thread and "the candles used for waxing it," etc.

But the most complete and authentic list of the laces made in the fifteenth century is found in the lengthy document, of which only the part referring particularly to lace is given here. It consists in a descriptive catalogue of the personal effects and furniture inherited by, and divided between, the noble sisters Angela and Ippolita Sforza, Visconti of Milan, and is dated September 12, 1493. To those who have read that lace was invented in Flanders or in Germany in the latter part of the sixteenth century, and copied and developed in Italy during the seventeenth century, the following lines prove how frequently assertions are made without proper research, and that as early as the fifteenth century, side by side with the pillow lace made by interlacing single threads such as was found in the graves of Achminpanopolis, and which received the distinctive denomination of *bone-lace* in Italy and England, existed the more elaborate and newer lace made with bobbins twirled in Paris and called, as to-day, "*fuxi*" and "*fuselli*," and all the varieties of needle lace specified in the pattern books published in the following century, as, for instance, *punto tagliato, punto tirato, rete a maglia quadra, reticella, punto in aria*, etc. Although, as will be seen from the Italian terms retained beside the translations in this fragment, the abominable orthography of the epoch, often strangely travestied the original name—

" One mantle of black satin trimmed around with gold tarnato (lace)."

" One veil in spun gold."

" Four small veils in silk; ten little veils in Neapolitan style."

" One linen sheet of five breadths worked in point."

"One piece of silver tarnato (lace) made in stars."

"One sheet of four breadths worked in radexela (net lace)."

"Four pieces of (net point) radexela to put on a mosquito net."

"One sheet worked with large insertions."

"One gold veil made in the Neapolitan style, with a gold cimosa (edging)."

"One gold veil made with an applied cimosa (edging) of black silk."

"One stomacher made in gold of grupi (knotted work)."

"One tarnato (edging) of gold and silk made in ossi (bone lace)."

"One stomacher of gold brocade with retini (net work)."

"One stomacher of red satin trimmed with gold work, a gugia."

"One sheet in raw silk of six breadths worked in radexela (net point)."

"One small bundle of various kinds of embroideries."

"Five pairs of sheets, one worked in radexela (net point)."

"One sheet of four breadths worked in radexela."

"One painted box with certain fittings of embroidery, made on veiling."

"Four pieces of radexela for a mosquito net."

"One knotted embroidery, on which were the pearls of my Lady Bianca."

"One broad radexela for a sheet."

"Six new pieces of tiny raxela (net lace)."

"Two tarnate of gold."

"One band worked *a poncto de doii fuxi*; (literally in point of two bobbins in contra-distinction to the bone lace named above)."

"Half of a bundle containing certain designs for the women to work."

"One sheet of *bombage* with certain fine workings; one sheet ditto, worked in radicelle."

That lace made with "pairs" of bobbins was a novelty is indicated by its being thus especially described in order to distinguish it from the older and simpler bone lace, and we have an illustration of it in the unpublished, authentic portrait in oil of Christopher Columbus, belonging to Cavaliere de Ferrari, of Genoa, of which we give a sketch, and which is the only portrait of the explorer in existence in which he is represented as wearing lace.

This quality of lace was made in Genoa and Spain, and is therefore most appropriately perpetuated on the collar of the man whose greatness brought lustre, wealth and power to the nation of his adoption, and added a glorious name to the long register of brilliant sons possessed by the classic land which gave him birth. But another historical character whom we must ever honor in speaking of Columbus has also left an impress on this lace. It will be remembered that when Queen Isabella of Castile joined her husband in the Spanish crusade against the Moors of Granada she made a solemn vow not to change her shift until that pagan city had submitted to the Cross. Many weeks passed and that historical garment assumed a very doubtful unbleached hue ere Granada fell. All Christendom at that moment had its eyes fixed on Spain in admiration of its enterprise and victories, and so in compliment to the Queen the new color was adopted for laces and frills all over Europe to such an extent that yellow starches were invented, and under the title of "Couleur Isabel" this shade of buff is still designated. This tint was especially given to the bobbin laces of Spain and Genoa, called "Gothic" whether made in silk or thread, of which, owing to its great fineness and antiquity, examples in a good state of preservation are excessively rare. The two pieces 628, 630 cases in buff silk belonging to Dr. Silvestrini are wonderfully fine and delicate in quality and design, and come from Spain, probably worked there by the Jews before they were expelled under the Inquisition. But Queen Isabella, beside the political cares and grave state questions which she never shirked, was a clever and devoted apostle of the needle and especially excelled in drawn work and lace-making, in which she also personally trained her daughters, so that the young princesses working with noble maidens under her intelligent supervision in the vast hall, consecrated to the use of the ladies of the Court, acquired her dextetriy, and when they married into England, Portugal and Burgundy carried with them the passion for this innocent and graceful art which they had learned to practice at their mother's knee.

Nos. 440, 442 cases are two pieces exquisite in design and execution of the same gothic lace, but this time made in Genoa. They have an especial historical interest for Americans, as they were brought to Perugia by a member of the Menicori Bracceschi family of which the distinquished and fearless condottiere of the middle ages, Bracciaforte da Montone was a member. The nobleman who first owned this lace was sent by the Pope as Ambassador to the French court and frequently passed through Genoa; and as the friends and family of Columbus were poor and industrious, it is possible that the fingers which introduced these linen and silken threads may have clasped the hand of the great explorer. Such thoughts cause us to touch with reverence these waifs of a bygone age and realize the truth in the words of Fambri, the great prophet of the revival of lace-making in Italy, in which he describes the gentle maids and matrons of the Renaissance mouldered to dust beside the heaps of ruins which once constituted the strongly fortified stone castles they inhabited, while the filmy work of their frail fingers lives on through centuries ever freshly adorning generation after generation of the human race in every part of the world to which culture has penetrated.

In the Milanese document of 1493 the most frequently recurring quality of lace mentioned is reticella (net lace or Greek point) and the process followed in its manufacture is described in our introduction. From a simple form of open work embroidery it rapidly developed into a perfect point lace; indistinguishable from " Punto in aria," it was a universal favorite all through the sixteenth century side by side with point and bobbin lace, the coarser qualities of reticella being especially adapted to body and house linen and Burato, for the working of which a complete pattern book was composed, is but a modification of it; but long before the publication of books of designs destined to serve as patterns for lace makers every household and convent had its sampler more or less complete, from which the stitches and patterns daily reproduced were copied by the women and young girls.

Nos. 97, 99, 101 screens are some of the more antique samples of this work, and No. 598 cases, which is of the sixteenth century, is an exceptionally large and beautiful sampler, and forms a complete illustration of the stitches used in this kind of lace. Punto Tagliato lies between Trapunto and Reticella, for it is like the latter excepting that a part of the linen ground is left visible as in Punto Tagliato, whereas *cardiglia* touches the other extreme and though appearing like reticella, is made entirely without linen.

We have enumerable examples of all these kinds of work, each one more beautiful than the other, and all alike interesting, for the Italian women of that period were quick to see its beauties, its possibilities of producing endless variety in effect and its advantages, as it did not alter at all in washing; so that in the super-refined extravagance of the Renaissance it was used not only to adorn sheets, pillow cases, towels and table linen, bedspreads, curtains and canopies with both insertions and borders, but the passion for it went to such lengths as to cause the bright colored walls of the summer apartments to be entirely covered with it, which a chronicler of the period says produced a dainty, cool and charming effect.

The Sforza document speaks of sheets of four and five breadths; this was because the old looms did not admit of weaving linen wide enough to cover a bed with one piece, and as seams are unsightly, pretty insertions were used to unite the widths; the tradition of this remains in Italy and in No. 656 cases is exhibited a homespun sheet such as is still in daily use among the Friuli peasants and illustrates these observations; the simple fact that I was forced to lend the humble possessor a sheet to take its place and complete her household linen during its voyage to America shows that such work is not there considered luxurious but simply neat.

No. 484 cases, is the heading of a sheet from an old castle in the neighborhood and other pieces exhibited in this group have served for the **same** purpose. Of course to match these sheets, pillow cases with reticella or bobbin lace borders and open work hems were necessary and universally in use.

No. 142 cases belongs to one of our peasants, and Nos. 130, 138, 478, 685 are all pillow-cases in the same kind of work executed at different epochs with more or less finess, according to the ability and wealth of the housewife and shaped to fit for centuries the heads of different ages of humanity from the cradle to the grave.

No. 286, 288 cases form the cover and curtains for a dressing-table, composed entirely of beautifully worked reticella parallelograms, which adorned a Tuscan bridal sheet of the fifteenth century and are e lged with fine antique Genosese pillow lace.

Nos. 334, 448, 602, 608, 610, 612 cases are several beautifully executed table-cloths, dresser covers and towels, all forming interesting examples of *reticella* and *punto tagliato;* each is different from all the others and some are adorned with pillow lace edges and fascinatingly complicated with tassels at the four corners.

Nos. 456, 462, 502, 504 ca es are also examples of Reticella and Punto tagliato, which have served on household and church linen and are now exhibited by the patronesses.

No. 463 cases is particularly worthy of attention on account of its fineness of quality, perfection of execution and the curious little doges caps and vases introduced in the design

No. 601 cases is also interesting as showing an entirely contrary treatment of the material and constitutes *Punto tagliato Reale*, the designs being cut out and diversified with graceful stitches, the ground being left in plain linen, a rare quality of work which can be perfectly reproduced at the school in Burano where the clever workwomen have recovered the secret of its fabrication.

Nos. 89, 109, 171, 283, 369, 389, 391, 399, 401, 403, 405, 407, 409, 411, 413, 417, 419 screens consists in eighteen samples of Punto Tagliato and Reticella exhibited on the screen, and as each one is furnished with the date of its origin and the name of the place where it was manufactured, no further comment with regard to them is necessary. No. 89 is of purely gothic design, and is the oldest piece of drawn work on this list. No. 397 is a fine example of the variety of lace called *cardiglia*, which, in appearance resembles Reticella, but is worked as in Venetian Point. These varieties of work are so beautiful, so characteristic and so little known out of Italy that they have been chosen to form the subject of the illustration representing the fashion of using lace from 1500 to 1600. This sketch reproduces an anonymous portrait, preserved in the Pinacotek of Bologna of a delicious, jolly baby of the olden times, literally smothered in laces lying wide awake in a monumental crib furnished with pillow, spread, canopy and curtains of this work, with even the corner columns swathed in bands of it; this lace introduced into strips of linen was also used alone or mixed with pillow lace for swaddling the babies of the Italian aristocracy as well as those of wealthy Hebrews.

The latter, however, in accordance with the prescriptions of the Talmud, were wrapped in bands diversified by quotations from the law, embroidered between the stripes of lace.

No. 320 cases is one of these, worked in Burato and worn to rags by several generations of Jewish babies, while No. 111 on the screen, and No. 314, 318, 320 in the cases have undergone the same process in the service of little Christians.

Nos. 554, 556 cases are two unusually long and richly worked bands of Punto tagliato and Reticella from Bologna, in a state of perfect preservation. They are edged with delicate, pointed Genoese lace, and cause us to regret that more of this artistic combination of needle and point lace has not survived the ravages of time. These two pieces exactly correspond in length, width and design with those on the canopy reproduced in the above mentioned sketch and may have served on this very crib or on that of some other little Bolognese aristocrat of the same epoch.

The list of laces in use during the fifteenth century, remains to be completed. We have reviewed the pretty ladies of the court, but have left unmentioned the queen and greatest beauty of them all; she enters last and all eyes turn to her as she ascends the throne of needle-work, from which no change of fashion has ever been able to banish her.

7

We stand in the presence of the earliest *Real Venetian Point*, called *Punto in Aria*. Since first invented this lace has ever enhanced woman's charms and men have been so attracted by its clinging grace that they have carried it upon their breasts and sleeves in court and camp, and sometimes dyed it crimson with their life blood, while the inordinate love of it has also played sad havoc with family coffers, so that estates have been mortgaged and whole families reduced to penury in order to satisfy the craving for its possession. Many laws have therefore been promulgated against it, but in vain. From its origin it was very expensive and the Venetian Republic tried to eliminate a fresh excuse for extravagance by suppressing it at the outset, and so in 1476 the Senate decreed that no Punto in Aria whatever, either executed in flax or in silver or gold thread should be used on the garments or on the curtains and bed linen in the city or provinces; but the women were accustomed to disobey the laws and it was necessary to rebel against the measures inspired by a desire to control their expenditure ,even though they knew it were for their own good. They had tasted the sweets of victory in their great rebellion against the Patriarch of Venice, Lorenzo Guistiniani, who had, in 1437, dared to forbid, under pain of fines and excommunication the use of costly jewelry and of every kind of superfluous adornments. But the women of that period, like the artisan of to-day, bravely "went out on strike," and refused to attend the churches until they had appealed to the pope. Their ambassadress must have possessed not only rich and becoming garments, but also an eloquent tongue and a persuasive smile, since she induced the pontiff to side with the women and to order the patriarch to cancel his injunction.

And when we observe No. 605, belonging to Signorina Angiolini, of Bologna, which is a framed example of this most antique Venetian point, which dates from about 1460, and resembles in its design some pure spirit flower, we can understand the woman excited over these exquisite blossoms of their inventive needles refusing to have the rare exotics destroyed by ruthless laws, and battling fearlessly to preserve the creatures of their mind and hand for their own particular adornment; they had at

once grasped the possibilities of effect which needle lace possessed and had realized that it added a needed delicacy to their
superb costumes through the twining of its graceful tendrils
in and out around the hems of their veils and coifs, and that its
soft white blossoms brightened by contrast the shell-like tinting
of their hands and necks and the rosy freshness of their cheeks.

PART IV.

The Golded Age of Lace. From Fifteen Hundred to the French Empire.

The love of lace developed into a passion during the sixteenth century, when all that was beautiful, formed crowds of faithful worshippers. The first artistic talent of Europe was inspired to compose designs for the complicated hand weaving with needle and bobbins, designs for which were published in book form and papers through numerous editions. Tradition has it, that no less a painter than the great Titian in person not only counselled his nephew Veccelio in the composition of his pattern book, but himself sometimes laid aside the brush and deigned to draw designs for a favored few. Reprints of the most celebrated of these pattern books published during the sixteenth century are to be found in the collection of books exhibited with the laces and the dedication of one of the rarest extant addressed to the Duchess of Ferrara. Princess Margherita d'Este, in 1592, is reproduced at the beginning of this volume, and showed how they were offered in homage to the highest ladies of the land, who gladly accepted the dedication considering it a great honor and compliment to the industry and skill of their households to be thus remembered. For in those days the daughters of many noble families were intrusted to their care for instruction in the arts becoming highborn womanhood, and each great house formed a kind of training school in literature and manners, which custom was replaced by the convents of the seventeenth and eighteenth centuries and the select boarding schools of to-day.

In the large hall or sala which runs the whole depth of the second floor of each great Venetian palace, an apartment which was formerly devoted exclusively to the women and their occupations, the mistress of the house caused the young girls to execute the wondrous works of skill and patience, copied from the pattern books, in which were often introduced for the easier execution of the design samples of the different lace stitches as in the unique example No. 614 cases, by Veccelio, which belonged for generations to the pious ladies of a picturesque old convent at Perugia, which has long been suppressed. There was a healthy spirit of emulation among the maidens of a household, each girl putting her whole soul and ability into the work allotted to her, for not only was she striving for a word of encomium more flattering than that earned by one or other of her companions, but all the women of one palace united in straining every nerve to have their work surpass that of some other great household, equally celebrated for its points. This rivalry among the women went to such exaggerated lengths as to give rise to insults and bitter quarrels among the men.

Princesses and queens complied with the industrious usage of the times and Catherine de Medici introduced the custom of lace work into the French court in the sixteenth century, just as the constant intercourse between the noble families of Italy and Spain during the fifteenth century had assisted the development and speed of varied lace-making in those countries nearly a hundred years earlier. This remarkable Italian woman, who had inherited the talent of her father Lorenzo de Medici, while directing the affairs of state, found time each day to spend several hours with the young princess and ladies of the court in the sunny work-room of the Louvre, looking out upon the river Seine. Here her daughter Margaret, the pretty, clever, giddy wife of Henry of Navarre, spent the most innocent hours of her life, embroidering the squares of reticella and net, which are called after her pseudonym of Reine Margot; see Nos. 310 cases and 415 screen, of this work; copies in the form of tea cloths are exhibited by the school of Brazza in the modern section.

Here also Queen Catherine's daughter-in-law, beautiful Mary Stuart acquired an inextinguishable love of French sunshine, gaiety and laughter, while deftly plying the needle, and when in her imprisonment she worked the veil (still religiously preserved), which framed her pale features on the scaffold, how sadly must the sweet memories of her happy youth and gay companions in France have entangled themselves among its threads.

The mother of Henry IV of France and of Navarre, Jeanne d'Albret, at her father's great castle in Gascony, had also learned lessons of application to the needle, and when she married Antoine de Bourbon in 1556 she gathered about her the noble ladies of Navarre, and in the following years of strife whiled away the many anxious hours caused by the persecution of her coreligionists in making, with the assistance of her companions, yards upon yards of superb embroidered net, part of which constitutes the bed cover, curtain and dressing valance, all edged with dainty gothic pillow lace, exhibited under numbers 168 and 170 cases. Net lace, or *Lacis*, being easy to work and not requiring great application has always been a favorite fancy work among high born lace makers, as is seen from the royal account books still preserved in the archives of England and of the continent. No. 150 cases is a beautiful piece of the earliest variety of laces which were made on the bias; it comes from Genoa, and is the property of Countess Gambaro. In it the net is edged with very fine Genoese lace worked in deep points. No. 662 cases is still older—it is a pillow case composed of squares of bias laces illustrative of the stories in holy scripture which treat of the virtues and the vices. It has illegible lettering, forming a border to each square, and the human figures represented are clothed in the costume of the Renaissance.

No. 94 cases is a towel or credence-cover, with either end formed by a very deep border of net, embroidered with unicorns drinking at a fountain.

No. 623 cases is also the end of a dresser cover, and repeats the same design of unicorns, although in this piece of work they are represented as supporting the arms of the proprietor.

In the sixteenth century the unicorns was a favorite design with which to ornament all objects used in connection with food, such as platters, cups, table linen, etc., because of the prevalence of the crime of poisoning at that period and the popular belief that the horn of the unicorn destroyed all venom; so that, though this fabulous animal never existed, a regular traffic was carried on in manufactured horns by the apothecaries, and the Neapolitan use of small carved horns or hands, with fingers pointed to conjure the evil eye, is a survival of the superstition. This foolish superstition originated in the legend of a poisonous lake which killed all animals that drank of its waters or birds that flew across it until a unicorn, passing that way, stopped to quench his thirst and the touch of his horn on the waters sweetened and purified them. Verses allusive to this were frequently inscribed upon cups, and there are many frescoes, tapestries and lace pattern books of the sixteenth century in the designs of which the unicorn is introduced. No. 94 cases is copied from one of these and executed with great attention to the harmonious combination of light and shade and to correct drawing. The above pieces, like all net lace of the same variety from Italy, are made in a straight band and edged with a *campane* of bobbin lace. The Germans, however, finished their oldest net laces with net teeth, edged with an overcasting stitch, as is seen in No. 625 cases, which is embroidered in the imperial eagles, with buttonhole stitch around the edge, because bobbin lace was not manufactured by this nation until long after net lace had become an object of general use. Little tassels were sometimes added in both countries to the turretted borders, as in No. 416 cases, which is a piece of Italian pointed net of the same period, and in No. 224 cases, which is a border formed of a very fine quality of Isabelle colored net most artistically embroidered in interlaced vines, among which cupids and dogs are portrayed as playing; it is edged with a fine *campane* and the graceful composition is in the perfect, harmonious style of the Italian art in the sixteenth century. This exquisite piece of lace belongs to the Santa Silia family, which came to Naples from Spain with Charles III.

No. 609 cases is of the same period made in silk and very effective. Owing to its brilliant coloring it is very coarse, and was evidently made for use on furniture and hangings such as we read of with minute details in the books of travel, and memoirs especially in those descriptive of Venetian luxury.

Another variety of net lace is called *Modena*. It is **not gener-**

ally embroidered, but the pattern consists in knotting the meshes together in different shapes.

No. 607 cases is an interesting example of this work, as in it squares of embroidered net and *modena* are alternated, while the border is entirely composed of *modena.* This variety lace has always been identified with Tuscany, and the peasants of to-day in the mountains around Florence use bed spreads and mosquito nets made of it.

No. 600 cases is a curious cover composed of squares of old Burato work alternated with modena, the whole being executed in cream and buff-colored thread of aloes. This was found in a sepulchre at Ferrara belonging to the marquises of Caliagnini, and is of the fifteenth century, though it is mentioned here because placed with the other work in net. Many other examples of lace have been found in sepulchres, and at one time a regular commerce was carried on between the natives of Corfu, Cyprus and the strangers on the steamers, which stopped at the ports of the islands, by means of the lace of rare beauty and great antiquity found in quantities in the sepulchres which they rifled. Many rich old Venetian families had settlements of wealth and power in both these islands, and though the places have returned to barbarity they still retain their absolute suzerainty over certain parts of them.

No. 107 screen is a curious needle lace of which we ignore the name. It was made for a short time during the sixteenth century, and must have been invented in Spain as its stitch resembles more closely that composing the Hispanomoresque head-dress than any other lace we have been able to find; it looks something like knitting or a lace so fine as to be out of the possibility of execution. It is, however, neither one nor the other, and is worked with a needle without a foundation composed of a textile, as is Venetian point, but also differs greatly from this, as it is made without the use of threads sewed down and then worked over to form the outline of the design, but is composed simply of counted stitches made farther apart or close as the design requires. No. 596 cases is a small table cover, the border of which consists of this lace executed in a design of alternate peacocks, emblems of jealous vigilance, and doves, the emblems of gentle faith.

Another lace which never had great success in Italy, but was very much admired in Spain and also in France, was the heavy silk guipure of the sixteenth century. This was made either in bobbin lace of silk alone in various colors, or mixed with metal or tinsel, and was also sometimes made in part or entirely with the needle. Its characteristic consists in a coarse cord replacing the narrow strip of vellum which was originally used, but on account of its brittleness was soon abandoned for the softer material; these were wound smoothly in silk or whatever other thread was to be used and edged with tiny loops; this gimp was then fastened down around the pieces of silk brocade or tinsel as is seen in Nos. 340 and 342 cases, or else close lace stitches were made forming flowers such as No. 75 screen, and at other times it was caused to curve about, following the design without being filled in at all, forming flowers, stems and arabesques, held together by loops. These Spanish guipures were sewed as decorative borders on heavy materials, such as velvets, cloths and brocades, but in Italy the people preferred to use embroidery where the lighter varieties of gold and metal lace and the delicate silk polychrome lace edgings were not appropriate; their fondness for color and appreciation of its values was greatly developed, as is evinced by the beautiful piece of the latter with a conventional design executed in pillow lace (number 80 cases) which is unrivalled by the most scientific combinations of the present day. Bu rato and Reticella were also executed at this period in colored silks mixed with thread, and added diversity of effect to the house linen.

No. 84 cases is a table cover of burato worked in colors; it is varied with net and pillow lace and edged with fringed pillow lace.

No. 328 cases is a band of the same work made into a bell-pull.

No. 82 cases is a broad band of cartiglia made of white thread and yellow silk in a Moorish-design of discs; it comes from Spain and is very rich in effect

In No. 332 cases a similar effect is produced by a fancy work which has of late become the fashion, in Italy and consists in sewing remnants of antique, white pillow lace guipure upon canvas and filling in all the space between the designs with Sicilian stitch executed in colored silks.

As already alluded to, the greatest period of intercourse between Spain and Italy began with the marriage of Ferdinand and Isabella and continued until the middle of the sixteenth century, when Spanish families had obtained dominion over the greater part of Italy and the Italian nuns imported into Spanish convents, and the Spanish girls educated in Italian convents exchanged with their new companions the knowledge of the arts of the needle as practiced in their respective countries. With France continual intercourse had already begun before the peace of Bologna in 1530, for in the early part of the sixteenth century Italy, full of beauty and art, became the coveted prey of all Europe and on its historic soil were fought out the battles for supremacy between France and Spain which in those days meant also Austria. The nobles and princes who commanded the invading armies on both sides carried with them the artistic spoils of its civilization, and all the laces and embroideries executed until the seventeenth century are copies of modifications of Italian designs.

Florence, Genoa, and above all Venice, as the most flourishing cities of the artistic peninsula, originated the fashions till the brilliant and extravagant court of Louis XIV definitely established the sway of Paris as the absolute dictatress of all which regarded dress. Notwithstanding the opening of the universities to women, which occurred in the fifteenth century, when a mixed college was established at Mantua under the direction of Vittoria da Feltre the Italian women did not develop into the kind of literary blue-stockings, neglect the feminine arts and spurn housewifely occupations. At Venice as early as 1414 Giovanna Dandolo, wife of Doge Pasqual Malipiero, whose intelligence enjoyed such wide-spread celebrity that the first book printed in Venice was dedicated to her, founded and protected large schools in which the productions of the bobbin and the needle reached such perfection that they assured the superiority of Venetian laces and obtained for them their great reputation at all the courts of Europe. The schools and ateliers opened by the benevolent woman after her death continued to spread the art among all classes of Venetians. The needle laces produced at this period in Venice as well as in Spain are generally known under the name of Spanish point, to distinguish them from the more elaborate designs executed in the same lace at a later period.

No. 659 cases is very antique and is edged with deep Spanish points; it represents the transition from reticella to punto in Aria, being destined for church uses and illustrating in fine stitches the Pasqual Lamb, emblems of the Passion, the gates of heaven, angels, birds, etc. (This has been reproduced at the school of Burano).

Nos. 515, 512 wall are photographs of some curious pieces of this quality of lace consisting of elaborate and complicated figures, composing entire biblical or mythological stories.

No. 308 cases is also very old and represents tiny figures of women; it comes from a convent at Udine.

No. 594 cases is a band of *punto in aria*, originally the property of an old family of Mantua.

No. 606 cases is a table cover composed of deep artistic reticella inserted in fine linen and edged with bobbin lace.

No. 283 screen is a piece of the same lace, placed in the screen beside No. 285, which is a modern imitation of it made in Switzerland by machinery, which has been very much the fashion for dress trimming during the past two years, but can be compared in no way artistical with the original.

Nos. 458, 460 cases are beautiful examples of *cartiglia* of the sixteenth century.

No. 456 cases is *punto in aria* of the same epoch, as are also Nos. 248 and 312. The latter consisting of an artistically designed deep lace composed of different sized conventional thistles. Executed in Spain.

No. 616 cases is another band of Punto di Spagna.

No. 126 cases is of interest as illustrating a special variety of Venetian guipure made during the sixteenth century in linen thread; it is executed partly in needle and partly in bobbin lace.

No. 216 screen is a second example of the above, executed according to a different design.

An example of the embroidery most admired in Venice during the sixteenth century, is furnished by the tablecover, No. 114 cases, composed of deep red antique satin and velvet richly embroidered in gold tendrils, intertwined with scattered flowers of delicately tinted silks, worked with the exquisitely natural shading and excessive fineness of execution, distinguished by the title of needle painting.

In 1557 another Duchess Lelia Dandolo, wife of the Doge Lorenzo Priuli who, like the gifted Dogaressa Malipiero occupied herself in benefiting humanity, merited by her noble character and charitable deeds, the unusual exaltation of being personally crowned, which was not accorded to the wives of all the Doges, but only to those who had individually distinguished themselves in such manner as to merit this the highest honor which the republic could confer. The costume the Duchess wore on this occasion is described as having been copied from that of one of her predecessors. The headdress consisted of a cap of gold bordered with deep Venetian point, from which hung to the ground a white veil edged with point lace, and the same chronicler relates that the great ladies and high officials' wives who attended the ceremony wore the immense collars of point lace spangled with gold, jewels and pearls which are seen in the portraits of the Medici family. These were supported by fine metal boxes called verghetti, which were manufactured in Venice in such abundance on account of the great demand for Venetian lace caps, collars and ruffs that the inhabitants of a whole quarter of the town were occupied in their production of them, made of every size and quality, so that the whole quarter came to be called dei Verghetti after them, a title which it still bears—others of the ladies at this imposing ceremony wore lace caps and lace *bavari* or bibs, for which so many designs were published during the following fifty years; others wore long veils edged with deep bands of *punto tagliato a fiorame* (the superb Venetian raised point literally translated sculptured point), and altogether the sight was of stupendous and unrivalled gorgeousness as all the cloud of lovely women preceded, followed and flanked by the high Venetian officials, standard bearers, nobles and pages, swept in grand and solemn procession under the procuratia, around the square before St. Mark's, and up the Giant's stair case of the Ducal palace. No. 244 cases is an example of the last named lace in the pure design which first characterized it. No. 166 cases shows the splendor to which it developed in the seventeenth century; this rich and rare cape belonging to the Countess Telfner was evidently destined to adorn the red mantle of one of the Doge's or one of the ambassadors sent out by the senate with special orders to dress in superb style, so as to prove to all who saw them how rich and grand was the proud Republic they represented.

No. 297 screen is a cuff made in Venetian *punto in aria*, representing animals (hares); it has the raised edge in use at the middle of the sixteenth century, as has also No. 611 cases belonging to Mrs. Cuthbert Slocomb, which is finished in deep Spanish points and composed of a running design with which the dogs of the Carrarese, peacocks, scorpions and eagles are intermingled. This is an example of the Carnival lace especially manufactured for grand occasions, such as marriages, births, etc., which always contained the arms or emblems of the great families in whose honor the celebration was to take place. To this flounce belong 16 oval pats such as were used in the slashed sleeves, of the sixteenth century; these together form a worthy relic of old Venetian costume which receives an added interest from the piece of fine bobbin lace, No. 174 cases, exhibited by Countess Passafava dei Carrarese, for this contains also the dogs belonging to the great family of Carrara and the quartering of peacocks used by them at that epoch, but this time combined with lions and foxes—so that the two pieces record different marriages in the same house, one in the sixteenth and the other in the seventeenth century.

No. 155 'screen is another interesting example of emblematic lace, and consists of deep Genoese points which must have formed the edge of some ruff or standing collar, and represent the crowned double-headed eagle of Austria, combined with a shield containing the white cross of the House of Savoy. The development of

Italian bobbin lace, also made rapid progress during the sixteenth century. First of all among them continued to rank the delicate conventional Gothic laces, which were modified into ever varied and new patterns, always retaining the same quaint effect, but following, however, two systems of design, the one being round and wheel-like, such as the Maltese and Moorish laces, see No. 620 cases, the other pointed like pine trees or the oriental date palm-leaf pattern which frequently composed the entire design. Of these latter laces No. 570 cases is a beautiful creation, and No. 282 cases is very gracefully composed in the form of a collar, edged with needle lace reticella. No. 574 cases belongs to the same epoch, as also Nos. 161, 185, 103, and many other examples on the screen.

No. 119 screen is the end of a towel with palm leaf insertion and a turretted border; both Nos. 121 and 135, also on the screen, have a graceful running design executed in the same lace.

No. 140 cases is a pillow case with a beautiful insertion of this lace forming conventional flowers alternated with inserted repetitions of the same design, which begin on the opposite side and fits into the space left between the triangular group of flowers; it is edged with a narrow insertion which repeats the same flowers and leaves in a simpler combination.

No. 165 and several other samples on the screen, which are all marked with the place of origin and date of manufacture, belong to this variety of lace, but it would be tedious to enumerate them here.

The Italian needle laces known as Punto Tagliato, Reticella and Cardiglia, were imitated with bobbins producing an almost identical effect, and wearing equally well on linen, whereas the fatigue and cost of production with the bobbins was vastly inferior to that with the needles.

No. 466 cases is an example of this lace, as are Nos. 129, 371, 135, 381, and many other pieces exhibited on the screen or introduced into pieces of household linen mixed with needle or other bobbin laces.

No. 231 screen is a simple insertion made in enormous quantities and used in sheets and pillow-cases and coarse underwear.

It was infinitely varied in design, and rude though effective borders were produced to match it, of which Nos. 145, 133, 137, 169, 175 on the screen and many others, such as Nos. 648 and 650 in the cases are examples. These were made in every part of Italy, from the Alps to the extremest point of Sicily. In Genoa the designs of this quality of lace, as well as of the others already mentioned, were influenced by Spain (see the guipure No. 613, and the table-cover No. 640); but the lace-makers of this city also learned an entirely different stitch from Malta, as is seen in the examples No. 167, the insertion Nos. 201, 319 and 385, the last having in particular a decidedly Moorish effect.

From the Moors the Genoese and Venetian mariners of the sixteenth century also acquired another kind of artistic trimming to which they gave the name of *punto a groppo* (knotted point), now called by its Moorish name of macramé. This complicated fringe, composed of five knotted threads, is equal to a lace in design and execution, and when treated with long threads wound about bobbins it becomes one. Signora Enrichetta Ruggi, of Padua, has composed an entire group (number 200 cases) illustrating the evolution of this kind of work from the simplest knotted fringe to the most complicated lace, and Countess Avogadio of the same city contributes a rich and interesting album (194 cases) of antique lace samples, containing an authentic bit of the original "*groppo*," which is very rare. This lace is made extensively around Genoa and is used to edge house and table linen, as are also the fringed coarser guipures and torchon laces, copied from those of the sixteenth and seventeenth centuries already mentioned (see Nos. 139, 193, 373) on the screen, which are original samples of these varieties of lace. In Venice and in Sicily and Naples, as in the countries and islands of the eastern part of the Mediterranean, the bobbin laces were affected by the trade with the Orient and developed designs resembling those for embroidering or braiding. The following are a few samples of these: 325 and other samples on the screen, as well as 490 and 128 in the cases, show the same character as Greek lace, which always has one or two coarse threads passing along the ribbon design which forms the pattern of the lace and is identical with modern Russian

and Hungarian guipure: 186 cases is the same kind of design but
different in treatment, having a mesh ground and thick cord following the Arabesque designs of the lace in the middle of which,
at frequent intervals, large holes are left to vary the monotony
and reduce the heaviness of effect, and here is found the wide and
original idea which developed into the beautifully fine Neapolitan
and Milanese points. No.321 screen is a sample of white and No.323
screen of yellow guipures which, as well as No. 150, are from Corfu
and are characteristic of the work produced on that island.   No.
328, however, is composed of the renowned fibre of aloes, in this
instance used unbleached, although in many of the finer laces it
differs only from white thread by its more silvery effect.   The
laces from Cypress and the southern islands of the Mediterranean,
as well as those from Madeira, although oriental in design (see Nos.
268, 508, 316 cases), resemble the cloister laces of the eighteenth
century which, though fine in appearance, were neither slow nor
difficult of execution and so were taught by the nuns wherever
they founded schools (see No. 106 and others in the cases).   These
oriental and Greek designs rapidly developed in the artistic
atmosphere of the Renaissance into very beautiful and costly
laces; the work-women adapting their advantages to the laces
they were producing whilst they entirely suppressed their defects,
and they, therefore, soon developed into the highly prized points
of Genoa, Naples and Milan, and into the beautiful guipures of
Rugusa and Venice, which have always retained the original
oriental character in their flowers and arabesques.   No. 222 cases
is a superb example of the ability of the women of Venice who
dedicated themselves to the manufacture of this kind of lace.   It
is a very deep flounce, composed entirely of tendrils, leaves and
flowers following each other in varied combinations of perfect
naturalness and grace, showing the subtlest art in the composition;
all these are formed by the convolutions of a ribbon of close
stitch, bordered with a fine cord, the tendrils being held together
by purled bars while the hearts of the flowers are composed of
fancy complicated stitches, also made with the bobbins.   This
flounce belonged to patrician family, Buoncompagni of Bologna,
and is said to have been made on purpose for the brilliant and

talented Pope Gregory XIII when he was still Cardinal Ugo Buoncompagni.

The Italian artist whose pictures most faithfully reproduced the embroideries, laces and splendor of costumes which distinguished this century was Lavinia Fontana, the daughter of a painter of Bologna. She was born in 1552, and was greatly protected by this same house of Buoncompagni from which she received frequent orders and the powerful recommendations and patronage of this great pope, and she died while working at Rome, whither he had called her. She not only enjoyed a deservedly great reputation in her own country (some of her paintings being so exquisite in drawing and execution that they have been attributed to Guido Reni), but her name was known far and wide, and the king of Spain ordered one of her pictures which occupies a prominent place in the Escurial palace. Other examples of the Venetian guipures she loved to portray, are Nos. 470 to 482 and 442 cases, a beautiful piece of this lace belonging to a lady of Genoa. Nos. 365, 359 and some other pieces of lace on the screen are interesting, as they are of a different variety of bobbin guipure, which is purely Italian in style and execution, and which is especially characteristic, as it has never been copied in other countries. Even in Italy it was produced and only about Venice, Ragusa and on the shores of the Riviera by the fisher folk, who destined it for the service of the church. We here designate it by the name of Rapallo, to which village, with the neighboring Santa Margherita, is attributed the earliest manufacture of this kind of lace, in order to distinguish it from the numerous other varieties of Genoese guipure. In the register of the Parish church at Santa Margherita exists an old parchment design for working this lace (which has been reproduced in the school at Brazza); it must be of very antique origin, for on the back of this design is noted a list of old fishing nets and laces presented as a votive offering to the church where it was found in 1592 by the fishermen, as a testimonial of their gratitude for a successful season of coral fishing. In No. 307 and among the samples, No. 652 cases exhibited by the nuns of the Ursuline Convent in Cividale in Friuli, who guard the only Longobard temple still existing and in 268—we have samples of this lace of which, a

8

beautiful piece is in the possession of the chapter of St. Daniels an old fortified burrough in the same province. The finest speci, mens are only to be found in the churches, but the government does not allow the religious bodies to send art treasures of any kind out of the country and we were too pressed for time to have these laces photographed. No more perfect example could be desired, however, of this rarely beautiful lace, than No. 146 cases, which, when it is made so very fine, is called vermicelli. Here the design is formed entirely of narrow cords or tapes no wider than drawing strips woven in the most difficult of all bobbin stitches to work continuously and with regularity, as is done here. This lace is placed at the foot and around the neck and sleeves and on the shoulders of a surplice where it is mixed with reticelles; the seams of this priestly garment are held together by curious buttons and loops, and it possesses a twofold historical interest, in the first place, because it belongs to the son of Angelica Bafic, the clever, noble-hearted woman of the people, who, in the second quarter of this century, devoted her entire zeal and intelligence to the reorganization of lace industry in Liguria, and whose name has become among the lace makers a synonym for thrift and intelligence; secondly because this antique lace and the Indian muslin, of which the vestment is composed, was presented to the great Carthusian monastery in Pavia by the Emperor Napoleon i. Who knows in what part of Italy that great collector and re-distributor of antiquities had picked it up?

In the wave washed villages where these laces were made, on the shores of the Adriatic, thrift and the fruits of activity were everywhere visible, or on the Gulf of Genoa, while the men were engaged in fishing, or on long voyages in the great Venetian and Genoese merchant vessels, their wives and daughters, who stayed at home, worked diligently with the bobbins or the needle, producing well paid laces, the price of which added to the family comfort or formed a sum destined for the daughter with which to start in housekeeping when the lover returned from the perils of the deep to claim the young girl whom he had courted during the previous winter.

The arsenals and foundries in Spezia and about Genoa combined with the work on the great fortresses and ports have modified the customs in Liguria, but this simple story is repeated year
by year at Burano and around Venice, thanks to the thrift of the
female population and to the prosperity produced by the earn-
ings and educational influences of the lace schools. The different
romances in the lives of the lace-makers have become with years
crystalized into a pretty tale about the invention of the fairy-like
"Rose point" "e se non e vero e ven trovato,"and worthy to be
repeated here to enliven the dry facts we recount.

It appears that at the epoch when every second woman in
Venice, rich or poor, was occupied in making lace, a sailor-lover
brought home to his sweetheart some strange and lovely growths
which he had been inspired to pick up in the depths of the sea
while diving to gather coral, thinking to give her pleasure. On
his return home he offered her these "frutti di mare" (sea fruits)
as the Italians appropriately call them, as a simple memento of
his summer toils and a proof of his faithful memory of her.
Shortly afterward he started on another and this time much
longer and more perilous voyage, undertaken that he might
obtain more rapidly the honestly earned gold which was necessary to begin in comfort their young wedded life, and in parting he
sought to console her with pictures of his glad return, and jest-
ingly warned her not to put out the fire of her bright eyes with
too much useless weeping, but to use it rather to guide her needle
in making such a beautiful wedding veil as would cause him to
find as smart a bride as any lord's awaiting him in Venice. Her
loving heart treasured up this jesting suggestion, and she determined to follow it by picturing in soft lace each simple gift of his
so that on her bridal day they would illustrate what had occupied
her thoughts during the many weary months of separation. With
true artistic talent and infinite patience she wove in finest thread
the reproductions of the tiny shells and of the frills and fluted
sea-weeds, the delicate sea-grasses, mixed with fairy-like reproductions of star-fish, sea anemones and urchins, and all the mul-
titude of marine gems, the whole being held together by delicate
tendrils copied also from growths of the great deep, so that when

the happy day dawned that was to crown their happiness by the union of their faithful hearts, this simple Venetian maiden stepped forth from her lowly home to meet her lover, blushing beneath her own handiwork, forming a veil such as no crowned head had ever been able to pride itself on wearing, and presented to the sunlight the first example of that rarest and most delicate of all laces, the inestimable "Rose point," of which many of the beautiful Venetian point laces (from 1033 to 1040) exhibited by Her Majesty, the Queen. are composed.

The small fichu No. 114, and the deep cuff No. 172 cases are such fine, complicated examples of this lace that they are worthy to be placed with their royal sisters to illustrate this romance of the needle. While the professional lace-makers toiled with inventive zeal, they were not forgotten or neglected by their high born patronesses of all that was beautiful. A Lady Mary of the great name of Morosine, which is synonymous with the honor and glory of Venice, had no sooner married than she devoted her lofty intelligence to the amelioration of her poorer sisters. She had ever been inspired oy a fervent desire to benefit her countrywomen, and made use of the experience gained in the women's workroom of her father's palace to start a school and large atelier, which she personally superintended, becoming one of the most severe and undefatigable protectresses of artistic design and perfect execution in the various Venetian points. Another daughter of the same house, also named Lady Mary, who married the Doge Marini Grimaldi, following the example of her ancestors, devoted her private purse to the founding and maintenance of a great atelier in the quarter of Venice called Santa Fosca, richly endowing it and providing a permanent teacher and directress, who was guaranteed every comfort and a pension for life. This school produced the clever workwomen who executed those beautiful laces, which tempted the wealthy of the whole of Europe, and which caused Cardinal Mazarin, and afterwards Colbert, to cast such envious glances on this source of prosperity for Venice; probably its busy workrooms were those visited and described by the French ambassador whom Colbert had instructed to spy out all details regarding the production of and the commerce in needle lace and write him a careful report of all he saw and heard, these curious letters being still in existence in the French archives of state, and probably it was here that this same French nobleman bought the very pieces of Venetian point which, he writes to Colbert, he is sending him to illustrate his statements and to serve as experimental patterns for the French in case the minister cared to try having them copied for the French workwomen. The directresses of this exhibit have been unsuccessful in their endeavors to open the ancient coffers of this great family, and draw from perfumed darkness some rare bit of antique Venetian point which would carry to America the memory of this old atelier, and of the many historic and philanthropic deeds in the history of the proud Republican city, with which the name of Morosini is inseparably associated in the mind of every school girl, but for all that there are no lack of illustrations furnished by great Venetian families.

The Countess Rapadopoli has contributed a rare collection of historical laces, which will be described later in this chapter, and the family of Falier, which has counted so many doges, ambassadors and senators among its sons, has had its historic laces photographed (Nos. 423,425, wall) for the ladies, and in them is seen interlaced among the delicate blossoms, of which consist the Rose point, the doge's horn and double F, forming the monogram of the personage for whom the lace was executed. Among the photographs the Cathedral of Lucca sends two, and No. 421, wall, of the same quality of rose point, which belong to its treasure; and the Princess Corsini, one of the queen's ladies, who is also a patroness, contributes a most interesting collection of photographs of the superb Venetian lace existing among the innumerable objects of art which form the heirlooms of that renowned Italian family, of which her husband is head.

The photograph, No. 441 A, is taken from an exceptionally elaborate piece of reticella, of the sixteenth century, composed of leaves and wheels, and edged with deep turrets.

No. 441 B wall is photographed from a magnificent flounce in Rose point of the seventeenth century introduced at regular intervals with a monogram and princely crown surmounted by a canopy, representing the special distinction of the "baldachino" (canopy) accorded by the pope to the Roman princes or noble houses as a mark of peculiar favor. No. 443 H wall is taken from some of the same set of lace and constitutes the lower end of one of the extravagant aprons which were the fashion in the seventeenth century and sometimes cost a thousand dollars. No. 443 B. wall represents a perfectly preserved square collar in the form of a jabot of the kind depicted as worn by Colbert in his portrait. This example is trimmed with richly worked "punto tagliato a fogliamo." No. 443 C wall is reproduced from a cuff and border of rich Rose point belonging to the same family.

No. 543 and the succeeding numbers to 571 are all photographs of Venetian embroideries and laces of this epoch still existing in the convents of the province of Udine not far from Venice. The patrician family of Rezzonico, of which Pope Clement the VII was a member, is represented not only by the superb Venetian point lace (1004) of the eighteenth century, belonging to Her Majesty Queen Margherita, and which has been so frequently copied at Burano, but also by a surplice, No. 196, in exquisitely embroidered muslin with insertions of pillow lace and bordered with choice lace of the kind made by the Salesian nuns. The piece of lace No. 386, near by, was also made by the nuns of the same order. Tradition says that this surplice was made for the Rezzonico Pope Clement VII, as an offering from his native city, and the admirers of the great poet Browning presented it to him in recognition of his love for Italy and Venice, and above all as a memento of the mighty pope, who, in his youth, passed musingly in and out of the great saloons and marble courts on Browning's purchase of the palace. This surplice is lent by the lady patroness, who now occupies the vast and solemn palace built in the childhood of that pontiff, and, which of late years became the last earthly home of the glorious poet, whose son she married.

No. 514 cases is another surplice and the most antique in this historic group. It dates from the sixteenth century and is composed entirely of bands of finest *Burato* worked in *trapunto* and trimmed with insertions and borders of Genoese point. It is the property of the old Bolognese family of Dallolio, a daughter of which has rendered its name illustrious by her poems.

Other beautiful flounces and bits of rose and different Venetian points which have been left unmentioned and can not be described for lack of space are:

No. 622 cases, a jabot of fine rose point.

No. 354 cases, a cuff of the earliest quality of the same.

No. 343 case, a square of elaborate rose point.

No. 345 cases, a cuff of the same.

No. 329 cases, a piece of ivory point.

No. 349 cases, a square of linen, edged with "Punto tagliato a fogliamo."

Nos. 100, 102 cases are two flounces, one of "Punto in aria," and the other of ivory point; they belong to the most flourishing period of this lace; and 266 e is interesting as having been made in the same lace, for the border of one of those immense handkerchiefs which necessarily supplemented the jewelled snuff boxes of the seventeenth century and are inseparably united with them in the depths of the voluminous pockets of the period. Finally we linger beside No. 256, a flounce consisting of the softest, most exquisite quality of Venetian "punto in aria" composed entirely of fine leaves and delicate tendrils. This was the favorite lace of Louis XIV, the same which Colbert sought all too successfully to have copied by Frenchwomen and to establish as a French product.

260 consists of the deep cuffs or "revers" worn by men and women alike at the period when it was made; and 258 is the narrow trimming of the same set of lace. This superb lace originally belonged to the royal house of Navarre, and is truly regal in conception, execution and effect. No wonder that on contemplating such work the wise statesman coveted for the industry of his country the well filled sacks of golden coin which were sent every year to Italy in exchange for such wonderful and delicate fabrics.

Ever since 1613, under the powerful and far seeing Richelieu, severe restrictions, followed by absolute prohibitions, such as the famous Code Michaud and the supplementary ones, which continued to appear from time to time, had been promulgated in vain against every kind of lace, one of these which serves as an example for all has been most wittily recorded in the satire called the " Revolt des passements," dedicated to Mademoiselle de la Crousse, Madame de Sevigné's niece.

But these wise laws, by which Richelieu, Mazarin and his pupil and successor, Colbert, tried to limit the terrible extravagance of the French nobility had been enacted in vain, and the fashion for lace was so great and the resolve of the wealthy to resist their decrees as obstinate as was their determination to follow the example of the young " Roi Soleil " and his gaudy butterfly court, who spent millions on dress and furniture. In fact, the young king was the first to defy the law, having inherited from his Italian grandmother an exceeding vanity and love for fine clothes, and above all an especial fondness for Venetian laces, so that he set a ruinous example to all those who surrounded him.

Note. This piece is very curious and full of information about the laces in use at the time of Louis XIV, and as it has not been given in any modern publication, we have considered it worth while to reprint it entirely, as an appendix to this volume, which will be sold separately.

This weakness of his was so widely known that a rich Englishman, desirous of ingratiating himself with the king, traveled in his private carriage all the way to Venice, where he had a wonderful hat manufactured, in the finest Venetian point lace, composed of soft, white, human hair instead of thread, to offer as a rare and becoming present to the youthful monarch on his coronation. This little attention is said to have cost the Briton forty eight thousand lires for the hat alone, without counting the expense, worry, anxiety and fatigue incident on a long journey with so fragile and precious an article at that period. As soon as Colbert could turn his attention to commercial questions his quick intelligence realized that the time had come, when laws could no longer restrain the tastes of the rich who would have their luxuries at any price, and that the only way to stop the steady progressive impoverishment of the country, by the exportation of large sums of money in exchange for rich merchandise, was to find a means of rivaling, with home products, executed by the same rules, the same material and effects, the alluring beauties from afar, for these Italian laces and silks, especially, seemed to bewitch all who saw them and to exercise a fatal attraction to reckless extravagance, and he therefore studied thoroughly the question of their introduction and prepared everything with minute care, and when he had found a soil suited to the coveted products, he started the inhabitants of Lyons at manufacturing the rarest qualities of silks and velvets and with regard to lace he managed by promises of great rewards and special favors to persuade skilled workwomen to come and teach their secrets to the far less able lace-makers of France. Mazarin had set him the example with more ordinary silks and with other trades, and Venice, who now saw her cleverest artisans slipping away from the workshops, was forced in self-defence to promulgate a severe decree inflicting imprisonment and even death on the families of those emigrants who should continue to absent themselves, but promising not only full pardon, but also honors and lucrative employment to themselves and to their relatives if they returned; but it was already too late, the barriers had been broken down, the habit established, cupidity on the one side and French intelligence, high patronage and the irresistible will of the "Grand Monarque," backed by the genius of Colbert on the other, had conqured, and the Queen of Commerce, whom centuries of prosperity had rendered lazy and negligent of her own interests, was destined to see her monopoly of the manufacture and trade in velvets and laces slowly ruined by the fierce competition, business enterprise and clever statescraft of other cities and nations.

Ten years of able management permanently established the manufacture of point laces in France. The exclusive right of manufacture had been ceded for this period to a society having such directors as Pluymiers, Lebie and Lebie de Beaufort, in whose hotel in Paris, the emporium for its products was first opened and where also the board met and Louis XIV went to examine the first French lace. The king's smile was, in those days, worth all the most attractive modern advertising, and the directors did all in their power to gain his approbation, and so when His Majesty went after supper to the Hotel Beaufort to see the new laces which had been made into carefully chosen designs, such as he was known to like, he designated them by the sounding title of "*Grand point de France*," and declared himself highly pleased with them, who, at court, could fail to be pleased also? and when soon after, he opened the wonderful new pavilions at Marly, each lady of the court, who was his guest on that occasion, found a complete garniture of this same lace awaiting her in her dressing room, as a delicate attention from the king, (a prize packet advertisement worthy of so great a personage) how could she fail to discard her old Venetian point and to wear instead the new lace in honor of the most amiable and generous of hosts, and when all the lucky women, who had been to Marly, wore French lace, how could the unlucky ones who had not been invited, appear in court in Italian point, as a perpetual reminder of their enforced absence?

Thus was floated a new French industry in the seventeenth century, and it strikes me that behind the highflown court compliments and graceful elegancies was hidden all the clever commercial astuteness of our work-a-day Paris of the nineteenth century. This intelligent stroke of business diplomacy is recorded by Borleau in the poem called " l'e pitre au Roi."

—"Et nos voisins fenstres de ces tributs serviles,"
—"Rue payait a leur art le luxe de nos villes."

The gains of the society were naturally enormous, but on the expiration of the monopoly it was not renewed, as Colbert desired prosperity among the people and a more rapid diffusion of the new industry than could possibly take place under even the most extensive of monopolies and, therefore, encouraged the forewomen in setting up manufacturies of their own. The society had started schools in Aurillac, Sedan, Duquesnay, Arras, Soudan, and other towns, but these places soon lapsed again into making the bobbin lace for which they had been previously distinguished, and it was in Alençon, and in the neighboring town of Argentan and surrounding villages alone, that the new variety of needle lace took root, and this is easily accounted for by the fact that the tradition of needle lace-making already existed there, while they were ignorant of the use of bobbins. Catherine de Medicis had received the county of Alençon as her dower and during her widowhood paid long visits to the castle where, courting popularity, she surrounded herself with ladies from that province whom she inspired with her love for working in reticella, embroidered net and the laces of her time, teaching them herself as she had instructed her daughters and the maids of honor at the Louvre. These ladies on their return home taught the new work in their turn to all their friends, and the fashion gradually spread through the neighborhood so that when Colbert, in 1665, began to look round for favorable spots in which to start the new industry, the intelligent Favier Duboulay, who, in his official position at Alençon had every opportunity for observing the condition of the industry, wrote to him that vast number of women and children in and around Alençon and Argentan were busied in producing "velin," which was what they called reticella, on account of the parchment on which it was worked, and a proof of its resemblance to the lace afterward manufactured is that this term was retained by them to designate the needle point which supplanted it. He also wrote that for several years a certain Marthe Barbot dame de la Perriere, "who had learned the art in Venice," had been perfecting so many of the able work-women in point lace; that there were eight hundred who were engaged on the finer qualities, and Mme. de la Perrieré was able to sell the products of her ateliers for which there was great demand at very high prices. It would seem that here the monopoly should have immediately and greatly prospered, but people were accustomed to working at home from too long accepted designs and resisted the innovations in every possible way until forced to submission by the government officials; they then learned to produce most beautiful work and through the company and the Italian teachers furnished by it acquired all the knowledge Colbert desired, which extended to eighty-five varieties of stitches. This story is less romantic than that told of Colbert's neice, the abbess of a convent near, and of his mooted castle of Lourai, in which Mrs. Pallisier says: "The manufactory was started under the direction of the

wonderfully clever, though mythical, Mme. Gilbert, who had at
great expense brought thirty lace-makers from Venice. Of this
country seat she, Mrs. Pallisier, even gives an illustration in her history of lace, where she also tells of Mme. Gilbert's visit to the King
of Paris, the rewards she received, etc., all very interesting but decidedly legendary, as the only shot necessary to fire at the frail
fabrication to see it crumble is to mention that the castle of Lourai did not come into the Colbert family until the prime minister's
oldest son, Jean Baptiste, married Catherine Therese de Martignan
to whose family this castle had long belonged and who brought it
as part of her dower in 1679, fourteen years after the opening of
the lace schools at Alencon by the company.

The lace which the women preferred to make at Alencon was
not the regular Point de Venise, although this was produced when
ordered, but the lighter Burano point which came into fashion
when that frail porcelain-like beauty, the Fontange, decided to
cover her skirts, as well as her head and her arms (she would
rather have died than have hidden her pretty neck), with rich,
though vaporous laces, wishing to enhance the light and airy
effect characteristic of her style of beauty.

Of course the old and fat ladies of the court immediately
followed the fashion and adopted this style of dress, and the
more severe Venetian *punto tagliato a fogliame* and Spanish points
that suited their vast and dignified proportions were abandoned
to the men and the priests.

Those little seventeenth century moths who aped the butterflies and fluttered perpetually about the fair flowers of the court,
and were known as "*abbes*," also preferred the lighter laces
adopted by the women, in whose boudoirs they eternally posed ·
and flirted. *Pupazze* or "*babies*," as they were called in England,
the great lay figures dressed in the latest fashions, were sent
every year from the French capital to all parts of the world, and
the costume of the Italian ladies was as superb as that of the
French court, as is seen by the gold embroidery, in No. 190 cases,
made at Florence and by the portraits of the period. French
lace was everything, the French fashions "*de rigueur*," and the ladies
who received Louis XIV at Bologna on his visit to Italy and

entertained and feasted him endeavored to appear more French than the ladies who accompanied him, as we see from the cartoons illustrating his visits there, of which we exhibited reproductions, for the costumes of this golden age of lace have been portrayed minutely, six times a year, from 1530 to 1796, in animated scenes peopled by celebrities and painted often by well known artists on large sheets of parchment in water colors, forming elaborate miniatures all bound in sixteen great volumes which are preserved in the state archives of Bologna. These form the illustrated *Insignia*, (a word derived from *cose insigni*, *i. e.*, things remarkable), and are the cartoons which accompany the records of the names and arms of the gonfaloniere of justice, and the eight *Anziani* or *"ancients,"* two for each quarter, or gate of the city, who governed Bologna for two months, and then were replaced by other nine of the most prominent nobles and citizens. It was the custom to illustrate the most important events of this short administration, and to this we are indebted for these most remarkable paintings. Now and then comes a sad note of pestilence or death, but as a rule we are treated to exact and minute reproductions of the great receptions, processions, feasts, tournaments, games, spectacles and religious ceremonies, in honor of some visiting prince or potentate. Here we see represented the black lace and deep *"point d'Angleterre"* flounces which Madame de Sevigne writes about as having just come into fashion under the name of *"jupes transparentes,"* and as so becoming and so bewitching. The fancy for black lace was so great at this period, when for the first time it came into use and was therefore a complete novelty, that *lace designs* were even stamped upon linen in black, and dresses trimmed with these borders to imitate the original and expensive new variety of lace which could not be manufactured fast enough and cheaply enough to satisfy the demand. A piece of this old fashioned "print" is exhibited on the screen No. 301. In the Insignia the deep flounces and black laces are worn by the ladies with *"coiffures a-la Fontange,"* that is to say, with their heads adorned with coxcombs of lace filled in at the back with feathers and exaggerated out of all semblance to the dainty lace kerchief which the beauty, whose name they bear,

tied so gracefully about her pretty head when the truant wind
played havoc with her tresses on one of King Louis XIV's hunting parties. These same Bolognese ladies in the *Insignia* have
dresses cut as low as they were worn at the French court, and
edged above the body and sleeves with lace or passement. They
wear long gloves and carry their muffs to balls and to dinner and
everywhere else with them just as did our "*elegantes*" three years
ago with their "boas" made of fur or feathers. We see these
muffs represented in the hands of the ladies at the banquet given
by the Gonfaloniere Francesco Ratta in 1692, which was so very
grand and solemn a function that every guest appeared with his
or her invitation carried in the hand as a card of admittance, and
judging from the confusion and disgusting faces depicted, there
seems to have been no end of jealousy, rancor and bad humor
displayed by the guests who were placed according to their rank.
It is from part of this cartoon the sketch has been taken illustrating the fashions from 1600—1700.

The muffs, the fontanges and the low-necked dresses accompanied their mistresses also to the solemn *aula* of the University
when they went to hear the wonderfully wise and equally youthful and beautiful Laura Bassi lecture on philosophy whilst the
more frivolous sought distraction from the elevated theme to which
they could or could not soar by ogling the men present who wore
quite as big wigs, stiff coat skirts and elegant cravats and other
lace furbelows and whatnots as their cousins who were at the
French court at Versailles.

It is to be hoped all these dressy Bolognese were patriotic
enough to wear the Burano point, from which the Alencon was
copied and had not imported all their laces with the fashions
from France as they did during the empire, for this old Burano
lace is so soft and beautiful that it truly deserved a better fate, as
Nos. 267, 269 on the screen, and Nos. 476, 308 in the cases
will prove, which are examples of this work left unfinished in the
convents by nuns long since dead. No. 308 cases is especially
lovely in design, with its tiny cornucopia full of microscopic
flowers.

Nos. 271, 273 screen and the collection No. 302 and 304

cases are pieces of it, many of which are in a ragged and neglected state, but still serve to prove the fineness and beauty of design and of workmanship which characterized old Burano lace.

No. 304 cases showing the shape of the sleeve falls made in the eighteenth century, and No. 266 *a b*, are exhibited by Signora Arca, of Padua, and No. 208, a flounce, and No. 214, a border, belong to the Countess Papadopoli, in Venice.

No. 436 barbes belonging to the Countess Biacceschi; they are all rarely beautiful pieces of this Italian lace and nothing from Brussells, Alencon or Argentan has ever surpassed it. That the ladies of Italy in the eighteenth century appreciated the French adaptation of their art is illustrated by the following lists of the laces which their descendants sent to the exhibition.

To begin with Alencon, as having been the first French "centre" of lace-making, Her Majesty exhibits in No. 1041 one of the trimmings, which started from the neck, reaching to the edge of the skirt, where it was lost in a pleat; these were the fashion during the reign of Louis XV in the eighteenth century.

No. 1042 is a cap and Nos. 1043, 1044, 1045, 1046 are all flounces of the same period. Nos. 1047, 1048, 1049, 1050 are all small pieces of the different laces which Her Majesty has lent to the School of Burano at different times to be copied and included among their models. Other ladies who exhibit interesting pieces of Alencon are the Countess Papadopoli, who contributes the jabot worked in tiny bees worn by Gerome Bonaparte, king of Westphalia, at the coronation of his brother, the Emperor Napoleon. It was presented to the Countess Angelica Aldobranchini by his son, Prince Napoleon, on her marriage with the great grandfather of the present Count. The reliefs in this lace, as in some of those of Her Majesty, are stuffed with horse-hair, this process being copied from the early Venetian point lace, but it is not pleasant to wear, as the sharp ends come out after a time, and Her Majesty had the horse-hair in some of hers replaced by thread packing at the School of Burano.

No. 212 cases belongs also to the same lady patroness, the Countess Papadopoli, and has a charming Louis XVI design of tiny bunches of flowers, held by bow knots.

No. 216 cases belongs to the same, but it is of the reign of Louis XV.

No. 272 cases is the same kind of lace exhibited by Signora Anais Forlani, of Padua.

No. 122 cases is a round cuff of the same lace exhibited by the patroness, Countess Colleoni, from the old collection in her family.

The piece of Point d'Alencon, No. 160 cases, belongs to the Countess Bonm, one of the patronesses, and was inherited by her from the Empress Maria Louise, through one of the Empress' maids of honor, who was an ancestress of the present Countess. It is copied in the design 48, made at Burano, which is a great favorite.

No. 520 cases are two broad scarf ends, and Nos. 564, 560, 568 cases are three trimmings of the same lace, and 572 cases is a pretty narrow edging of this French lace. On the screen are exhibited Nos. 275, 277 and a bit of machine made imitation, No. 279, for comparison with the real antique or modern Alencon point. In Alencon the lace manufacturers, with the producers who worked for them, sold everything in their own name, and went entirely on their own reputation, and objected to any one of that city receiving the special privileges attendant in those days on the title and position of purveyor to the king. But at Argentan two or three ateliers enjoyed the coveted title, and most of the laces for the use of the royal family, and especially for the royal trousseau, were made there. Her Majesty, the Queen of Italy, possesses the most beautiful existing examples of this lace, and exhibits the following pieces of Argentan point:

No. 1001 of the royal laces is an immense bed cover which is used by the princesses of Savoia during the ceremonies and receptions following the entrance by their royal offspring upon the stage of life. It served in the room of which Her Majesty sends a photograph at the birth of His Late Majesty, King Victor Emanuel in the Carignano palace at Turin.

No. 1002 of the royal laces is a deep flounce, composed of a pastoral design containing ladies swinging, and is said to have been designed by Watteau, and served with No. 1001 in the rich decoration of the princess' apartments.

Another deep flounce of this same lace, No. 1003, is designed with illustrations of animals taken from Æsop's Fables.

No. 1005 of the Royal laces was made especially by order of Napoleon the First, as a present for Cardinal Retz and No. 1008 among the narrow flounces is the trimming that matches it. This lace represents great medallions containing flowers and doves on a fine tulle ground held together by bows and garlands of ribbon on a large mesh ground. It illustrates the innovation which was introduced in 1807, and consisted of shading the flowers, one petal being made in close stitch and the other in sheer stitch, and gave rise to a tremendous amount of criticism, but had so lovely an effect that it permanently established itself in lace-making.

Another Royal Alencon flounce, No. 1006, has a design of balustrades and stairs and vases, such as was very much the fashion in the floriate rococo decorations of the first half of the eighteenth century.

On another flounce, No. 1007, are represented grasses and swans, and from No. 1009 to 1020 are all pieces of narrow Argentan lace, many of which have been also lent by Her Majesty as models to the school at Burano. Among these pieces Nos. 1011, 1012, 1013, 1014 are particularly interesting because they are shaped to form the bertha-like trimming worn around the shoulders which was first introduced by Madame de Maintenon as we see by her portraits, and No. 1019 is one of the rich frills for elbow sleeves which were worn with the same costume. Among other ladies who exhibit pieces of this beautiful lace are Mrs. Hungerford who sends No. 164, which is composed of a design of lakes and bridges in the finest possible quality of Argentan, the meshes of the ground being entirely made in button-hole stitch.

Nos. 180, 182 cases are pretty examples consisting of two barbes and a trimming of one design. In this lace Marie Antoinette loved to adorn her delicate beauty in all that was softest and lightest and the world followed her example as she was literally the queen of fashion in the eighteenth century, accepting the position seriously and holding long and serious consultations

9

with Madamoiselle Bertin, the greatest milliner of the epoch, who was called to Versailles for the purpose of consultation, as would have been a real prime minister, but to decide grave problems of shades and forms instead of political questions, and then on her return to Paris this assistant or mistress would publish the autocratic decrees of fashion laid down by her sovereign and from which there was no appeal. This queen, surrounded by her family, has therefore been taken as the subject for the sketch representing the prevailing fashion in the use of lace during the eighteenth century.

Her above mentioned love of airiness and simplicity is that which she obtained by the use of Indian mull and the embroideries upon it which resembled lace, such as No. 257 screen and were called Broiderie des Indes, but even these were not light enough to satisfy her fancy, and so she is said to have originated the lace composed of designs in fine linen lawn, delicately worked around the edge in lace stitch and held together by bars as in the Venetian Point; an example of this variety, No. 262, belongs to Mrs. Orville Horwitz; at other times the mull was applied to a ground composed of all the sixty-five varieties of Argentan stitches as is seen in the flounce, No. 96, which seems the embodiment of the graceful Royal Pastorales at which the youthful queen played in the Park of Trianon and awakens a sigh for the untimely extinction of so artistic and charming a being.

No. 292 cases is a veil, most artistically embroidered in thin lawn dots, on the finest "point de Paris" which was a variety of the bobbin lace made at Malines, engrafted on the coarser pillow laces made about Paris in the seventeenth century and producing a wonderful hybrid. This veil belonged to the Empress Marie Louise as did the soft laces, Nos. 294, 296, which were worn by Napoleon with the three jabots (300), one of which is worked in roses and the other two in lotus flowers and leaves, evidently in honor of his Egyptian campaign. Another piece of lace, which belonged to the Empress Marie Louise, is No. 298, an exquisite example of fine Valenciennes, and was also made when everything Egyptian was the fashion in France.

No. 178 *a* and *b* and 278 cases are other examples of point de Paris belonging to different patronesses.

Many other thread pillow-laces were made in France beside the blondes of Normandy and the tambour laces of Brittany, such as No. 297 which variety was composed of designs embroidered on tulle net, in chain stitch, darning or simply the design of mull being applied on the tulle as in a sample on the screen. No. 364 is a veil, from Spain, of tambour net embroidered with the royal crowns, an F and a 7 being alternated in the design. It was made for the wife of King Ferdinand, the Seventh, Queen Christina, and belongs to Lady Layard.

Nos. 154 and 296 in the cases, and No. 331 on the screen, are of the same kind of lace from Italy. The French laces in the style of Torchons, were made in the mountains at Lepuy, and the same laces were also produced in large quantities in Italy, Switzerland, Germany and many other countries of Europe, and have been of late largely produced in England and Ireland.

The laces in the style of Valenciennes were made on the seacoast at Dieppe, Havre, Harfleur, etc.; the deep and finest qualities of pillow-laces, resembling those of Belgium, were made principally at Chantilly (118 cases) and at Mirecourt, Arras, Bailleul and above all at Lille in the north. No. 280 and 472 cases are of a particularly fine quality of Lille lace, and the latter belongs to the reign of Louis XVI, during which it was very much the fashion as were all the Flanders laces from which it originated.

In Germany the art of bobbin lace-making developed in the sixteenth century, but it has only been of late years that needle-lace has been produced in any quantity by the Teutonic races. Anysburg was the center of international trade at the time of its origin, and therefore in most frequent communication with Italy and Belgium, and here pattern-books were first published in Germany, and the surrounding country became the German center of lace-making.

Barbara Ultmann was a native of the neighboring Nuremberg, and when she married an engineer director of the mines at Annasberg, in the then wild district of the Hartz mountains, she found the miners' wives about her new home making nets of bone lace, such as that found at Panapolis, and she undertook to teach them the more perfect bobbin lace she had learned at home as a girl. Her pupils were apt, and the industry grew with immense rapidity under her intelligent direction, bringing money and civilization to the inhabitants of the entire province in which was situated Annasberg, and when she died in 1575 at a ripe old age, she was mourned by no less than thirty thousand workwomen, who owed to her their knowledge of the new industry, and the sixty-eight descendants, consisting of her children and grandchildren who accompanied her body to the grave, fulfilling in their number the prophecy of a gipsy who had foretold to her that for every stitch she taught the people, God would send an increase to her family. The story must have grown out of the coincidence, but it is firmly believed in all Saxony and Bohemia, where her name is greatly revered, and her tomb at Annasberg is often visited, and a superb statue has been raised there to her memory of late years by public subscription.

The Huguenots and Protestants who took refuge in Germany, Denmark, Sweden and England assisted in the development of the manufacture of pillow-lace, wherever they settled down, as it was the handiest means of self-support and was a means of lucrative gain both in selling the results of their own industry and by teaching the secret of their production to others. In England the spead of lace making was facilitated owing to the yearly distribution of prizes to encourage the perfection of this class of handiwork. In Ireland, as in all Catholic countries in which lace has been introduced, the nuns first taught it to their pupils. In Scotland, Elizabeth, Duchess of Hamilton, tried in 1745 to establish its manufacture with small success and after her death its production nearly died out. Pieces of lace and samples from all these countries, as well as from South America and Ceylon, are included in our exhibit, but marked with the name of the country in which they were manufactured, as these qualities exerted no influence upon Italian lace making. With Flanders it is different. Its wonderfully even and superior quality of flax and thread had enjoyed a great reputation in Italy as early as the thirteenth century, if not before, and were used entirely for the production

of fine linen textiles and lace-making in Venice. In the latter
part of the sixteenth century the Netherlands furnished Spain
with most of the laces used in that country and was always the
most celebrated source of fine pillow-lace, but I have not had
time to find out how this art developed to the transcendental and
complicated finess of quality it reached in the most expensive
laces of Binche and Brussels where it took a clever workwoman
a year to produce half a yard of edging three inches wide (such
as seen in numbers 124 and 270 d), and hearsay is a weak staff to
lean upon unless well supported by documentary evidence. In
any case, during the seventeenth century the manufactory of
these filmy airy laces began which have never been equalled by
pillow laces from any other part of the world.

In Holland and Belgium each town had its specialty in lace,
which was attractive and different from that of any other. Brussels, the capital of all, worked both in needle lace alone in the
style of Burano (as seen in No. 270 A cases) and in pillow-lace
alone resembling the oldest Mechlin lace (see No. 212 cases), and
in Point d 'Angleterre which is a mixture of these two kinds of
lace. It was originally invented for the English market, hence
its name (see No. 251) which with the laces surrounding it on the
same'leaf of the screen, illustrate the varieties of fine Flemish
lace with the exception of No. 247, which is old Devonshire edging copied from the Dutch laces called Trolle Kant, No. 259,
which is Cretan peasant lace, the machine-made imitation of
Brussels, and No. 261 of old Mechlin placed with the other laces
for comparison.

The city of Brussels has been able, until the past year to hold
the dominant position in the lace trade, despite the enormous
size of the commercial centre of Paris and London; but rumors
from Belgium announce that it can not continue to stand the
competition of the rest of the world, because its workwomen are
paid much more than those of other nations, who have learned
the secrets of its art and will not resign themselves to lower
salaries.

Her Majesty exhibits in Flanders laces a superb flounce made

at Binche, No. 1025, and No. 1021, which **is** a large bed spread
strewn with designs of flowers and butterflies in Flanders point.

No. 1022 is a scarf of Brussels needle point.

No. 1023 is a cap of point d 'Angleterre.

No. 1024 is a deep flounce that matches the Flanders bed
spread with butterflies and flowers.

Nos. 1026 and 1027 are trimmings for a costume, consisting of
a bertha and the lace to match, and No. 1028 is a barbe of old
rococo Flanders lace, sometimes called Brabant point.

No. 1029 is a pair of the lappets often used instead of the veil
in the court dress prescribed by etiquette, and No. 1030 is an
edging.

All the above laces belong to Her Majesty.

Other ladies exhibit in Point d 'Angleterre and Flander's
point.

No. 108 cases, is a fine long veil, with Apollo represented playing on the harp and surrounded by birds belonging to the
eighteenth century composed of Flanders' point.

No. 110 case is a deep flounce with birds of paradise and swans
made in the same century and with the above and No. 111 cases,
a narrower flounce, forming a complete set of this beautiful lace.

Nos. 92, 90, cases are trimmings of Point d'Angletere.

Nos. 158 and 202 cases are of the same, belonging to the Bar-
oness Treves and the Countess Pautucci and No. 206 cases, is of
historical interest consisting of a deep flounce with double heading especially made at Brussels of "applique," Point d'Angleterre
for the Queen of Westphalia to wear at the coronation of the
Emperor Napoleon the First, and is worked in the arms of her
husband's kingdom. This piece of lace was presented by Prince
Jerome Bonaparte to the Countess Maddalena Aldobrandini
Papadopoli of Venice.

No. 360 cases is a flounce of Point d'Angletere.

No. 436 cases are lappets in old Brussels pillow lace of the
finest quality.

No. 518 cases is a veil in Point d'Angleterre with a design of
holly leaves and berries made at the beginning of this century
for the English market and brought from this country to Italy.

No. 520 cases are two lappetts in Point d'Angleterre, belonging to the Marchesa Grimaldi of Bologna, and are worthy of the name they bear.

No. 558 cases is a flounce composed of very graceful designs in the same lace, and No. 560 cases is an antique Brussels applique flounce, while No. 572 cases is a veil in old Brussels point.

Nos. 578 and 580 cases are two trimmings of Point d'Angleterre, and No. 624 cases is a jabot.

No. 220 cases, is a baptismal veil of the period of the empire, adorned with human figures executed in Point d'Angleterre, which belonged to Queen Carolina, of Naples, sister of Napoleon and wife of Murat, and was inherited from her by her great granddaughter, Countess Guerini Pepoli, of Bologna. Its design is unique and very artistic, although more suited to embroidery than lace.

At Binche were made the cobweb laces. Nos. 394, 396, 452 cases, etc.; at Malines or Mecklin, the delicate narrow flowered flounces and ruffles dear to the heart of graceful Marie Antoinette.

At Ypres and many towns were made the fine and solid Valenciennes; at Bruges, soft silk and thread laces were produced in simple, graceful designs, such as Nos. 362, 180 cases, etc., and the beautiful Flanders choir lace (see No. 242 cases) belonging to Marchesa Fianetta Doria, who is the directress of the branch of our committee at Genoa, and one of the Queen's Ladies.

At Antwerp a special style in laces was adopted such as the Troll Kant (see No. 438), and the Potten Kant(of which examples are also exhibited) which was suited to the plaited caps of the Dutch housewives of high and low degree, and every town had a new variety on and on, through the long list of Dutch cities and villages which each produced a perhaps less celebrated but always pretty lace, manufactured for home consumption alone, or else for exportation in vast quantities to England, France, Italy and above all, Spain. Those laces which consisted of a guipure, with a broad bold design were made in the north and the province of Hainault, and resemble the same quality of lace made at Genoa and Milan (see Nos. 104 and 120 cases). The pretty *rococo* designs came from Brabard and were so perfectly

reproduced in northern Italy where they were very much appreciated that they can not be distinguished (see Nos. 268, 368, 474,
480, 498, etc., in the cases, and 327, 223, 177 made in Friuli, on
the screen). The style and manner of producing these laces has
been described in our introduction and the frequent reproduction
of the simpler qualities combined with the immense quantities of
finer qualities which are still treasured in Italy, are illustrations of
the esteem which Flanders laces have always enjoyed in this
country.

There are some Italian bobbin laces which are worthy of being
placed beside the beautiful needle points already described and
the pillow laces above mentioned. These laces are all artistic,
and have a style of their own; they originally served as models
for the early Flanders laces, as they existed before them, but are
quite different from the airy, fairy products which were produced
in the Netherlands during the latter half of the seventeenth and
the eighteenth century, which we have just been passing in review.
They are, however, well suited to adorn the rich stately type of
Italian womanhood, personified in the Roman matron draped in
deep hued velvets and heavy satins, they also harmonize with
the solemn chants and rich decorations of Basilicas frescoed by
Giotto, and with altars from which gaze down the pure Madonnas,
painted by Raphael. The Italian designs for pillow laces never
pictured pastorals, etc., and so were specially adapted for
church linen and vestments as well as for personal and household decorations, and the prejudice against the introduction of
human figures or animals survives among this people.

Milanese point like the Venetian guipure originated in passement and developed rapidly into a superb lace at the end of the
sixteenth century.

The lace made in the Abruzzi resembles the Milanese point
lace which is made with a mesh ground, whereas, the Milanese
guipure and the Genoese guipure are indistinguishable; all the
pieces of antique guipures which have a very florate design are
ascribed to Milan, and all those composed of arabesques to
Genoa.

Her Majesty exhibits two pieces of Milanese point, No. 1,031 being a deep flounce of the finest quality of this lace with a design composed of vases and lambrequins and No. 1,032 royal laces which is a piece of trimming of a different design.

Other ladies have contributed the following Milanese laces:

Nos. 226 and 262 cases are flounces with flower designs.

No. 284 cases is a square sixteenth century collar.

No. 396 cases is a pattina used in catholic church ceremonies.

No. 406 cases is a fine flounce exhibited by Countess Agostini Venerosa della Seta, directress of our committee at Pisa. This is old convent work.

414 is a trimming of the same, and 588 is a handsome flounce of this same lace of which there are several other pieces and samples in the cases and on the screen, such as 127, 157, 205, 213, 375 and 235.

The following Neapolitan laces are of the quality known as old Abruzzi mentioned above, which are so named from the mountains between Rome and Naples, in which they were manufactured and in which a large production of inferior laces continue, only requiring the breath of revivifying commerce to bloom forth in their original beauty.

No. 218 cases is a flounce composed of a design consisting of flowers issuing from vases, conventionally treated and made at the time of Louis XIV; it belongs like so many other laces to the Countess Papadopoli.

No. 398 cases is a beautiful, fine piece of the same lace which was made during the sixteenth century in a convent destroyed by the ill-famed Marchese Ruffo, the terror of his country.

No. 3,404 is a flounce of a very fine, close quality, exhibited under the patronage of the Countess Agostine della Seta, and shows to what perfection and regularity, lace making was also carried in this part of Italy.

No. 338 cases is a piece of the same kind of lace bought in Spain; the design, which is coarse in quality, consists of the imperial Austrian double-headed eagle of the time of Charles V, and of a marquise's coronet. This Emperor conceded to several Italian, as well as Spanish, families as a sign of great distinction and most especial favor, the privilege of bearing the imperial arms, which are often repeated in the design books of the sixteenth century; and this lace was evidently made for some such personage. It belongs to Lady Layard.

Nos. 209, 219, 229 screen are all examples of this lace made in Naples, and Nos. 215,217, 227 are of the same lace, but made in the Abruzzi. At Ischia black silk laces such as No. 289 were made; at Offida, in the province of the Marche, much Abruzzi lace was formerly made, as also a kind of blonde in thread (see No. 274 cases) and all the ordinary antique household laces, as in every province of Italy; but now the production in the Marche has fallen to the very lowest quality.

In Venetia, besides the guipures with coarse cords, a lace was made resembling the Milanese guipure. No. 618 is an example of this lace, with which a surplice is trimmed. It has the antique trefoil design, which was universally made in Friuli in the eighteenth century, and No. 348 is an exact reproduction of the same design, made by a clever old Venetian lace-maker named Victoria Tranquilli, who also reproduces "blondes" to perfection.

In Fruili all the ordinary laces which were made elsewhere in Italy were also produced, as well as an original quality resembling old Swedish and Danish lace. (See No. 187 screen, Nos. 152, 380, 464 and 660 cases.) At Palestrina and Chioggia, near Venice, there was such a large production of torchon lace that Palestrina divides with Cantu the honor of having this quality of lace called by its name. Chioggia is identified with a certain starred mesh (see No. 131 screen, No. 410 cases, etc.), which is used with great effect even in the finest of Belgian pillow-laces. There is much variety in the simple old laces and an appropriateness of design to the uses for which they were destined, and many examples of them are exhibited on the screen and in the cases, but it is useless to enumerate them here. No. 336 cases is a table cover composed entirely of samples of the antique Italian laces; it belongs to Mrs. Bronson, who also sends a complete collection of samples of the ordinary modern laces made at Palestrina and the other islands around Venice.

The Ligurian, or Genoese, guipures have four entirely distinctive characters, forming really four different laces. The first, or Hyspano-moresque and Maltese variety, has been treated of with the Gothic laces, and we have also examined the second, consisting of the vermicelli lace from Rapallo and Santa Margherita. A third is identical with Milanese guipure (see samples Nos. 123, 125, 141, 151, 201, 377 on the screen, and Nos. 370, 374, 390, 392, in the cases). The fourth is different from all the other varieties of lace and is called "fugio" (*i. e.*, I fly), as it is very soft and airy. It is an adaptation of a guipure, consisting of broad ribbons of weaving, with open-work holes introduced as variations held together by a very few fine bars, the arabesques being combined in such a manner as to touch frequently and to obviate the need of extraneous supports (see No. 333 screen). The Countess Pigrone Gambaro, of Genoa, sends two beautiful flounces (Nos. 246 and 250 cases) of this lace. No. 408 is a flounce of the same, as is also No. 496, and many other examples which are to be found in the cases.

With the exception of the blondes we have now passed in review all the laces of Italy. Those soft, alluring, glistening, clinging tissues, ever beloved by the daughters of Andalusia, who remained faithful to them when the fickle fashions of France, which had created them in the seventeenth century, abandoned them entirely in the eighteenth, so that the world forgot their origin, and when these laces reappeared they became known by the name of the country of their adoption as Spanish blondes, which they have retained, although now principally manufactured in France and Italy.

The white and colored blondes, with metal introduced of the quality generally encountered, lack that softness of material and grace of design combined with durability, which are the chief attractions of lace. (As an illustration of this see Nos. 444, 446 and 590 cases.) But some of these hybrid laces compensate by their splendor for the defects of their less artistic sisters. Of these Lady Layard exhibits the following superb collection, placed together in the cases, which she made during her sojourn in Spain:

No. 346 *a* and *b* cases is a piece of antique blonde and with it is placed a modern copy of, it, made as are all the following copies of other silk laces by Victoria Tranquilla, of Venice.

No. 348 is the most beautiful combination of white silk and silver which could possibly be made, and consists of a broad scarf of artistic design in blonde lace.

No. 350 cases is a rose blonde trimming in white and silver.

No. 352 cases is a blonde lace scarf worked in white and silver in a design of the rose, shamrock and thistle, which form the emblems of Great Britain.

No. 354 cases is another blonde lace scarf made in white silk and gold thread with a design of flowers, grasses and tassels.

No. 356 cases is a blonde lace bertha in white silk and silver thread.

Nó. 358 cases is a white and silver blonde trimming. Other ladies exhibit blondes composed entirely of white silk, which were the rage in Italy under the empire.

No. 582 cases is an entire empire costume, including a mantilla composed of this quality of lace. It belongs to the Countess Grabinska of Bologna.

No. 584 cases is another costume of the same lace which was worn by Princess Maria Malvezzi Hercolani, Lady of The Croce Stellata, and Lady in Waiting at the Vice Regal Court of Prince Eugene Beauharnais in Milan.

Nos. 586 and 590 cases are flounces of white silk Blonde lace worked with a curious honey-combed ground, through which a coarser silk passes. These soft silk blondes, with their supple folds and great splashes of reflected light, have a certain attraction, and in any case the Italians owe them a deep debt of gratitude, for they alone carried the traditions of lace-making among the Venetian, Ligurian and Cantuese women across the sad years of overwhelming taxation and foreign oppression which for Italy composed the first half of the nineteenth century. These Italian blondes of inferior quality kept the bobbins flying, and though there was no demand for new point laces, the mending of the antique ones belonging to the Cardinals and churches kept the needle plying according to the traditions of the past, and that sufficed as a foundation for the intelligent revival which began on the Ligurian coast about 1848 with the production of a pretty lace resembling Lille and Mecklin lace, which was well suited to the style of costume then worn. (See the pieces Nos. 280, 412, 422 in the cases, 432, a cape and No. 516, a flounce, belonging to the Marchesa Cavriani).

When the fashion changed about Genoa and at Cantu, the lace-makers began copying the white and black Brussels laces, of which No. 254 is the first piece of this quality made at Santa Marguerita, Liguria, in 1868, for the Countess Pignone Gambera from a design she loaned the workwomen. These laces required great exactness of execution and re-developed the intelligence and ability of the workwomen, so that if the demand for Italian lace should increase in proportion to the cleverness of the lace-makers and the good will and necessity of the poorer classes, Italy is prepared to become in the twentieth century what she was in the sixteenth—the guiding genius of good taste in this art and the purveyor of the most truly beautiful laces sold on the markets of Europe. For though greater regularity may be found in the coarse laces of other countries than exists in those of Italy, even the most ordinary of her bobbin laces, if only the designers be allowed to follow the old traditions, possesses in company with the unrivaled needle laces the quality of true artistic sentiment, which gives them the prestige of originality, for they are not *modern lace.* This term is distinguished from that of *antique lace* being simply synonymous with mechanical perfection and a strict imitation of natural effects not applicable to this art. The finest modern *hand-made* lace is composed of perfectly even machine spun silk, thread or cotton, dyed a beautiful black, or bleached to a dead white, or colored a brilliant yellow *creme,* worked with wonderful manual dexterity in nicely shaded designs copied from drawings of real birds, butterflies, flowers and fruits, interspersed with meaningless scroll work or devices quite as applicable to cast iron, which are vulgar and tawdry in effect even on cafe pavilions; and how much more inappropriate to so delicate a fabric. The component parts of this quality of lace are all worked separately, one woman making the cast-iron devices, another all the roses, another the butterflies, etc., so as to obtain great

individual perfection at a sacrifice of artistic completeness; for no
two human beings can execute work exactly similar, and the difference between the execution of different parts is easily de-
tected by the expert. These pieces are then united with perfect
exactness, placed upon a machine net or needle-made ground and
carefully pressed out, producing a quality of work which has no
individuality or artistic imprint as had the antique laces, and could
be substituted by the productions of machinery; and but for a
lack of durability in these latter, no one but the starving lace-
makers deprived of the means of earning a livelihood would be
the loser.

As will be seen from the reproductions of old designs exhibited in the Italian section, both in the Woman's Building and in the
Palace of Liberal Arts, the Italian lace-makers have an indestructible sentiment of art and are capable of producing really
antique lace with all its inimitable forms and rich soft tones,
with the advantage of strong, new material and an unlimited
supply, productive of a consequently reasonable price well suited
to the present requirements of artistic homes. But, alas! side by
side with the enchanting evidences of what can be done with properly trained artists are placed pieces of laces which prove the
lack of intelligent guidance and the ignorance of the poor neglected
workwomen who toil unceasingly at starvation wages exe-
cuting designs they cannot understand, striving to follow foreign
fashions which are already extinct, and to ape the ever-changing
productions of great factories in flimsy imitations copied with
defective, puerile drawing, instead of reproducing the lace found
on their own old household linen, or that which they kneel before
each Sunday in church, or which is brought to them by their
priest to be mended, and which tradesmen buy up at any price to
sell again in countries where it is appreciated and sought after with
eagerness. Until now the artisans have neglected their oppor-
tunities as they have been neglected by those who should have
guided them; but in the past twenty-five years a new era has
been initiated for the home and art life of the lower classes, just
as it has begun for the entire nation in the realization of its aspirations toward liberty and unity. In each great city and in-

dustrial center, schools for artistic and manual training have been opened side by side, or in connection with the public schools; and in those dedicated to the education of the girls, not only all the household industries and usual professions but decorative drawing and lace-making are taught, and even in small, out of the way villages in the more advanced and prosperous provinces industrial night schools are springing up where higher instruction in agricultural theories practically illustrated and science applied to industry are gratuitously taught, so that the village artisan and the poorest peasant may alike learn to improve their methods of working, while their wives and daughters are taught the simple laws by which the sanitation and economical administration of their homes may be assured. A sunny day is indeed dawning for all the industries of Italy; the morning glow has already risen above the Alps and streamed across the land, and will be found reflected from the objects described in the following pages, and the bright day star which has long ridden high in the heavens, predicting the sunny future to the lace-makers, has been the far-famed, co-operative school of Burano.

PART V.

The Modern Lace.

(Its Artificers and Framing.)

The Italian section containing the historical and modern lace herein described is situated near the southwestern entrance to the Woman's Building, at the World's Columbian Exposition, held at Chicago in 1893. All the great palaces of which it is composed are designed in the style of the Renaissance, in honor of the Italian explorer, the fourth centenary of whose discovery of two continents this vast International Fair has been organized to commemorate, and the Italian directresses considered it appropriate to furnish their small section (which is entirely occupied by the lace exhibit) in the prevailing style, and it therefore represents an Italian sala, or salone, of the sixteenth century, the cases destined for the rococo laces alone having been made to suit their contents. In Italy women do not carve furniture, and the man who seconded the ladies and has furnished so beautiful a framing for the art treasures sent across the seas, is Cavaliere Valentino Panciero Besarel, of Venice. He is an artist of a type which belongs to the same period as the designs he creates.

The Italian Renaissance is bred in his very bones. He is the son of a carpenter who was also a wood-carver and a genius, and who lived up to the traditions of Venetian art, although his home was situated in the remote village of Zoldo, among the first spurs of the Dolomiles, those glorious Italian Alps which have ever been fruitful in artists. Here Panciero Besarel was born, and from his childhood determined not to abandon the trade of his father which was inherited from a long line of honest ancestors, but to climb the heights of art, ever faithfully following in the footsteps of Andrea Brustolon, the greatest of Venetian wood-carvers. Like many an American millionaire, like all the best artists of the sixteenth century, he began his life working at the hardest and most menial accessories of his trade, struggling with every nerve to obtain the pittance which would suffice to maintain him whilst he should study at the School of Design in Venice, so as to change his dreams and his aspirations into an art; and like them he succeeded. But the love of the beautiful and the good, the striving forever after an unattainable ideal, are sure to breed the sentiment of patriotism, which is so often the fore-runner of persecution, and even martyrdom, and this above all in Italy, the country whose atmosphere is so saturated with beauty, poetry and art, that strangers love to linger there and ever return, trying to call the land their own, while liberty and a desire for a united country is the dominant passion of every true Italian heart, and has inspired all the rebellions against foreign usurpation, which have at last been crowned with merited victory.

The young Besarel was like other geniuses, and so when despotic Austria, who had purchased the dominion over Venice with money levied by heavy taxation laid upon her citizens, sought to lure the young Besarel with offers of high honors and rich emoluments at Vienna, he turned a deaf ear, and sent his work to the Exhibition of Florence, where his faithfulness and talent were rewarded by a medal and sales to the amount of 6,000 francs, which procured him only fresh persecution, as he devoted the entire sum to assisting his unhappy countrymen in emigrating from under the foreign rule. In 1873, however, after the freedom of Venice, well-merited success at last crowned his effort, for his well-established reputation obtained for him a great order from the Prince of Wales; and since that period he has received gold medals at all the expositions in which he has taken part and been knighted, and the recipient of flattering honors from Austria, England and Italy, and from the French Republic. He has always remained the same simple child of nature and of art, although his curly locks have been bleached by time and by a terrible accident which deprived him of part of his right hand, which for all that "has not forgot its cunning." In the spacious

10

salons of this palace on the Grand Canal, which are crowded with
the children of his hand and imagination, he is visited yearly by
all royalty embassadors, and the highest in Italy; and even Her
Majesty, the Queen, orders of him most of the artistic furniture
and libelot with which she loves to surround herself, and never
stays in Venice without visiting his studio. The lady patronesses
who know him look upon him as a friend, and therefore naturally
turned to him in getting up their exhibition, as to the o.. who
would do honor to the faith reposed in his generosity and his
good taste. His pretty daughter trips about the place with all
the charm of an old-time Venetian maiden, and her smile is as
attractive as that of the delicious little cupids she sculptures, for
this demure young lady, who cannot count twenty summers, has
inherited her father's talent, and it is to her clever hands we owe
the modeling of the lace-maker, who sits so peacefully beneath
the great crucifix carved by the cavaliere, and is dressed com-
pletely in clothes the material of which was grown, spun, woven
and sewn by the industrious peasant women of Fruili.

The flax used for the underclothes worn by this lay figure was cultivated and spun by
Maria Puggarino, aged twenty, of the village of Ceresato, and cost ten cents. The lace was
made at the school of Fagnnia by a girl thirteen years of age, named Giudita Lestani, after
learning six months, and cost twenty cents. The dress is composed of silk refuse plucked from
the branches on which the cocoons have been spun by the silk worms cultivated at Brazza, and
is used to make home-spun hunting suits and most durable garments by the peasants. The
carding, spinning, dyeing and sewing of the dress and furnishing of the necessary adjuncts
cost $3.20, and is all the work of Arenellina Zanor, aged about twenty-three, who also wove the
underskirt and chemise, which with the material cost in all $1.90, the cutting out and sewing
which was done by Amelia Cervezzo, of Fagagna, for thirty-five cents. Amelia Cervezzo also
made the picturesque rug and cord slippers worn by the peasants when working in their houses,
the entire material and execution of which costs thirty cents.

The woolen stockings are made from the wool of sheep, belonging to the Michelet family
of Fagagna, which was carded, spun, dyed and knit into stockings by Angela Michelet, aged
seventeen, who also made the garters customary in her village, costing fifty cents. The woolen
shoes called zoccoli are hand-made by the men of the family, and those exhibited were executed
by Guiseppe Peris of Fagagna for thirty cents, the work in carving the wood costing ten cents
and the work in leather twenty cents. The peasants always buy their aprons and kerchiefs
unless they make them in crochet work, and these form the great objects of luxury in their
costume, costing in all when of the quality which is exhibited about $3.00; the lace on the
apron is made by Ernesto Schirati, of Fagagna, aged thirteen, and cost sixty cents. So that
the entire Sunday outfit of a well-to-do peasant amounts to the value of about eleven dollars
made in the most durable of materials, but to them it costs much less, as the greater part of it
is made of unsalable materials prepared at home at odd moments. The lace over which the
figure is represented as busied was mounted on the pillow and made by the peasant girl, Italia
Canciani, aged fourteen, after ten months' instruction in the school of Brazza; and everything
connected with the figure has been produced by peasants whose families frequent this school
or the branches of it which have been established in the neighboring villages.

Casa Besarel forms a charming household, and while I write, the words of a cultured American lady ring in my memory as she descended the worn marble steps and entered her gondola, which floated idly before them on the lazy blue waters of the Grand Canal.

"Thank you; you have not only shown me the most artistic carving I have ever seen, but you have led me back into the Venice of the middle ages. I felt it almost sacrilege to take away anything from where it stood, for all seemed part of a picture and so *unshoplike!*" Alas, the only fault of Besarel is that he is an artist and "unshoplike" and will leave his children richer in honors than money, forming a great contrast with many of the modern "Merchants of Venice," who go so far in their chase for foreign gold as to pay the gondoliers, couriers and guides, who conduct the wealthy strangers to their doors.

Signorina Besarel is not the only young Italian girl who has contributed her work to grace our exhibit. Signorina Costa of Rome, the daughter of the artist whose wife is one of the lady patronesses, has passed many busy hours over the painting in Italian "tempera" of the Renaissance, garland of flowers which forms the frieze about the sala, while Signorina Celotti of Udine executed in old tapestry painting the Album destined to contain the samples of laces made at the Brazza lace school, for which she has a kindly affection; and as if goodness and beauty were synonymous, all three of these industrious girls are so pretty that it is only a pity their clever work cannot be rendered still more attractive by their photographs.

The green silk, the soft lustre of which adds beauty to the laces within the antique carved furniture and causes those of Her Majesty to appear like white caps of fluffy foam upon the beautifully tinted waves of the Mediterranean, was spun, dyed and woven by women, in the silk and damask manufactory of Signor Domenico Reiser e Figlio, which was founded in 1848 in Udine, who also exhibits an album containing a few samples of the rich damasks and velvets here produced, which are exact reproductions of the celebrated antique Venetian silks, and are sold as they come from the loom, without any preparatory dressing and therefore quite indestructible like those which have survived the wear of centuries to adorn our drawing-rooms.

The gracefully wrought iron gate, transparent as a curtain in black guipure, through which the visitor gains admittance to the Italian section, as well as the album full of beautiful designs for antique wrought iron objects and for those made in chiselled metal, is the handiwork of Antonio Lora of Trissino, another typical Italian artist. His father was a carrier between his native village and Vincenza, and apprenticed his son at eighteen years to a wood-carver established in that city, whence the young man soon moved to Verona and finally, attracted by its art traditions, to Venice, where he maintained himself for twelve years by hard work whilst he studied design at the Academy and perfected himself in "niello" (one metal incrusted in another) and the lost art of casting a "cire perdue," so that Guggenheim Richetti and all the merchants of antiquities found a constant use for his talent.

During this time he also modeled the bronze medallion, erected at Venice to the memory of Sirtori, one of Garibaldi's most celebrated aides-de-camp, who was a native of that city, and his works carried off prizes at the universal exhibitions of Vienna, London, etc., as well as in the national expositions.

The beautiful gates in wrought iron of the museum at Turin are his handiwork, as well as others in London, Odessa, Frankfort, Berlin and even in the United States ; and for an amateur of Paris he has executed a perfect copy of the beautiful grating which surrounds the celebrated monument of the Scaligers in Verona. This work in *niello* is equally pure in conception and beautiful in execution, and it cannot fail to prove interesting to whoever visits Vicenza and finds attractions on studying the life of the middle ages, to take the superb road out across the laughing plains and the high bridge over the roaring Agno to the old fashioned peasant house, with its big courtyard full of cackling hens, surrounded by low, long rooms out of which the family has been crowded by the products of the master's art.

Antonio Lora, in metal work, like Besarel in wood carving, is as much an artist of the Renaissance as were the great examples whose work they seek **to** emulate, and both belong to **a** type which has survived the hurry of the nineteenth century in classic Italy alone; and to stand face to face with the life led by genius in the past, one need only seek Besarel among his pupils **on** the Grand Canal of Venice, or Antonio Lora in the simple smithy at Trissino, frowned upon by the bleak ruined castles of the proud Montecchios and haughty Capulets, which in former ages smiled on the loves of Romeo and Juliet. Here, like his proto-type Vulcan, this master of the anvil limps about among his workmen helping them to twist the glowing iron into artistic flowers and tendrils and the exquisite forms of lanterns, gates and balconies, products of his creative genius which the great dealers in bric-a-brac sell as treasured remains of old Italian art, for triple the sum paid grudgingly to their creator. Above the courtyard and behind the busy forge rises a hill crowned with superb gardens, terraces and greenhouses, in the middle of which stands the beautiful castle of Trissino, which forms the summer studio of Countess Loredano di Porto, the woman most distinguished in photography in Italy, whose works are known far and wide **for** their wonderful artistic grouping and perfect execution, and have won her the gold medal at the International Exhibition of pho-tography at London and elsewhere. She exhibits (42) groups posed to form genre pictures, which speak for themselves; and when we offer the best our land produces; can our visitors com-plain of the restrictions which limited space has caused us to place on the quantity of this branch of woman's work to be sent to America? The mother of this gifted lady, the Countess Bonin, another of our Lady Patronesses who lives on the oppo-site side of Vicenza, protects an industry which saves from want **the** unoccupied women of all the villages of the "Seven Com-munes," the inhabitants of which are the direct descendants of the ferocious Cinibians, who could boast of having routed two great armies composed of the flower of Roman **valor,** and of having yielded at last to the effects of the bad climate, **not** the attacks of the civilized soldiers who killed them **as they** struggled, lashed together against the overwhelming sunshine **on the** southern slopes of the Apennines. This lady sends **two** albums and three hats made of plaited straws in **the** Commune of Marostico and its neighborhood, where all the women and girls, with infinite ingenuity and ceaseless industry although poorly remunerated, twirl and plait straw instead of flax and hemp into laces, which are afterward sewn together, forming hats or exported to foreign countries where they are much prized for their lightness and solidity.

Another Italian lady, the Marchesa Negrotto Passalacqua of Genoa, shows that she has inherited the talent of her ancestresses. She exhibits a great table cover, bed quilt and the front of a gown worked by herself alone, in unbleached thread in the quality of lace called punto tagliato a fagliame before which all must pause in admiration, and realize that if the poor lace-makers were only guided by such refined and artistic talent as she possesses, they would produce, perforce, superior work, and that we may say what has been already accomplished in this line. We will turn to the schools, as it is in these that the lace-makers are trained and that the ladies of Italy seek to improve the quality of the work produced by cultivating the taste and ability of the young girls. These institutions are divided into two distinct classes; *i. e.,* those which are organized as co-operative societies, for which the pupils are permitted to continue to work after their training has finished, and in which they enjoy an augmentation, or suffer a reduction in the price paid for their productions as the market fluctuates ; or else the merely industrial school, which trains the pupils for a limited period, selling the better work produced by them to help maintain the institution and provide instruction for as many girls as possible. But once the pupils have left these schools, they are forced to provide personally for the sale of whatever they may produce, or enter the private establishments in which the trade they have learned is followed.

We will begin with those schools founded and directed by the **Lady** Patronesses, because the most important exhibitor is the **co-operative** institution of Burano, which sends over ten thousand **dollars'** worth of lace to Chicago.

SCHOOL OF BURANO.

The four hundred industrious and merry girls whose **hands** have gaily worked these beautiful needle laces while they sang the sweet snatches and boat songs of Venice, are now sorrowful, and the whole school mourns in silence for the intelligent, the good, the beautiful, the pious Countess Andriana Marcello, who for years has been its guardian angel and whose last work for them was to plan, a short three months ago, all the details for their share in this wonderful exhibition at Chicago. The golden cord of her sweet life has been snapped and she has been prematurely called to enjoy the reward of a life spent for others. The echo of her funeral dirge has scarcely died into silence and the ripples caused by the passing of her mourning barge across the laguna, which for so many years she followed to and from the school at Burano, have hardly broken upon the shore of that desolate island. The emotion of one who for the past six months has worked daily, guided by her experience and noble rectitude, and who in turning to each branch of this exhibit finds proofs of her activity, leaves me without words that could picture our sorrow; but the visitor who gazes on the sweet loveliness of Andriana Marcello, contained within the frame of simple black velvet which is placed near her beloved laces, will realize all that Her Majesty the Queen, the committee of directresses, the school of Burano and *Italian womanhood have lost with her.*

It was Paolo Fambri who first thought of raising the poor fisher folk of Burano out of the abject squalor into which, through years of misery they had slowly sunk, and which was rendered deadly by the fearful winter of 1872, when the frozen lagoons presented a stony breast, on which they beat in vain for bread. He first tried having nets made in large quantities for exportation as they had enough of these already, but other fishing communities made their own, and so his kindly heart caused him to divine the talent for lace-making, which lingered in the nature of the people; and seeking out old Cencia Scarparola, he found in her the embodiment of the tradition and he decided with the help of willing minds and hands to revive the art for which the island was once renowned.

The patricians of Venice seconded him with both sympathy
and money, and among them he chose two of the noblest as
of the most beautiful, both since ladies of the queen, both patronesses of this our new enterprise, to carry across the seas the
work of these girls who have been redeemed from a life of misery
by their own efforts, properly directed by these wise protectresses.

The princess Maria Giovanelli, with her long absences from
Venice, could not carry on the work she had undertaken with
such enthusiasm.   The young widowed Countess Andriana Marcello saw in it the realization of a dream long cherished by her
noble husband, and threw herself heart and soul into the work,
which she carried on with unabated energy for twenty years.
God has blessed her faithfulness, and Burano with is six thousand
inhabitants is now bright, prosperous and contented, and has
drowned the horrors of 1872 in the tender smile of its foster mother
the Countess Andriana; but she is gone forever, and it depends upon
all who admire noble, untiring devotion, to continue the work which
she has founded and organized so perfectly, that its only necessity is a steady affluence of purchasers, and that out of our abundance we buy to trim our gowns the delicate work of these
intelligently guided girls, rather than less artistic or machine
made lace, which last but for a season, and cannot remain with
our jewels to adorn the forms of our descendants in the happiest
hours of their lives.

All the designs of Burano lace are taken from the best antique
models, and Her Majesty, who as Princess Margherita di Savoia
accepted the honorary presidency of the school, has allowed the
superb crown laces to be copied there and never trusts them to
other hands for repairs.   For this reason and because they can
bear the most rigid comparison, these laces are placed near those
of her majesty, and each one copied from a royal lace is so
marked.   The beautiful bridal veil, which alone we have space to
mention here, is reproduced from the historic flounce of Argentan given by Napoleon I to Cardinal Rets, and design No. 5, according to the numbering in their price list, is copied from the royal
piece of Rezzonica lace composed of Venetian point, which has

frequently been duplicated by order of crowned heads as a wedding present to present to royal brides.

SCHOOL OF COCCOLIA.

Another co-operative school, but younger and much smaller, was founded by a lady patroness the Countess Maria Pasolini, in 1884, at Coccolia on her vast possessions in Romagna. This property is situated near the picturesque historical town of Ravenna, and she sends a collection of photographic views of some of its principal points of interest. It is here that lie the ashes of the immortal Dante, where he spent many of his years of exile; and it was here that in his footsteps long lingered the sweet inspired and discontented Byron, whose happiest hours were spent in his adored and adoring Italy. The cultivation of the fertile plains forming the surrounding province of Romagna, of which the inhabitants are a sturdy and independent race, is conducted on the system called in Italy "mezzadria;" that is to say, the proprietor furnishes the houses and the land, the peasant dedicates himself unpaid to the cultivation of the latter, and the two equally divide the profits. The population increases rapidly, and the superfluous members of the family must seek occupation by emigrating to some new farm, which is constantly being formed by the detritus of the rivers, or become laborers. The men have therefore organized in co-operative societies which undertake important contracts in other provinces and neighboring nations, and these are executed with rapidity and exactness, to the complete satisfaction of those who employ them, and the mutual benefit of all parties concerned. The Countess Pasolini, who is as intelligent and active as she is charitable, has thoroughly studied the economic questions of her surroundings and has published the result of her observations in several pamphlets, which have been reprinted in the first periodicals and were considered so important by French economists as to deserve translation, being invaluable and unequaled authorities for consultation on the subject of which they treat. The Countess in following these researches observed that the weak point of the whole system, above mentioned, was the disoccupied life lead by the women and

girls belonging to the families of the laborers. There are no factories around Ravenna, in which to employ superfluous hands,
and there is no economy in this day of machine-made stuffs to be
found in home spinning and weaving unless the first material is
produced on the farm; and so the Countess decided on founding
a lace school for the female children and these women, permitting them to work at home as soon as they became proficient in
the execution of the finer laces, which they learn to make with
great facility as they share the artistic temperament of the whole
Italian race; and the products of their industry copied from
antique designs are worthy of the exquisite velum album, filled
with rich satin leaves on which they have been placed to be sent
to Chicago. The school of Coccolia deserves encouragement,
and besides its album exhibits all too few pieces of its beautiful
work, preferring to execute the complicated designs for which it
is deservedly known in filling orders to running the risk of having
expensive laces left long unsold.

SCHOOL OF BRAZZA.

A still younger school is that under my direction founded at
Brazza, near Udine, Friuli, on September 8, 1891, at a small show
of peasant products and industries held at our country home by
the seven communes which surround it, with the object of developing the small household industries and thus forming a means
of accessory occupation and emolument for the large peasant
families during the long winters when the ground in this part of
the country is frozen or snowbound. Six girls, of which four remain among the best workers of the school, had been personally
instructed by me for only ten days in the rudiments of the art
and did such justice to their intelligent natures and powers of
concentration whilst working before the visitors the day of the
fair, that the vast public remained enthralled and could not be
persuaded to move on, and the jury of the exhibition decided
that this handicraft was adapted to the requirements of this part
of the province. Since then three schools have been opened in
quick succession, forming the clover leaf chosen as trade mark for
products and emblem of these modest institutions, and a fourth

small leaf is budding which promises to bring the proverbial good luck if only the children continue docile and industrious, and the public lenient to their defects. The oldest of the baby schools has scarcely doffed its swaddling clothes, though a brave and sturdy little one, for on its first birthday the precocious infant with its younger sisters had a hundred pairs of hands at work twirling the bobbins for broad and narrow laces at the big peasant show at Fagagna on September 8, 1892, and therefore received a diploma for cleverness and good conduct, while many of the busy little hands closed over small pecuniary prizes which gladden the hearts of proud parents and teachers. In fact, the infant develops with such unheard of rapidity and consumes such large quantities of pins, thread and bobbins, upon which indigestible articles it thrives, that it quite frightens its mother, who must appeal to all the friends of honesty and industry to buy the ever increasing products so that a lack of food and occupation may not stunt the child in its happy growth. The girls who attend the home school and its branches vary in age from seven to twenty and when they are seen twirling the bobbins and merrily singing in chorus the musical catches of Fruili, or seated under the great chestnut trees of the park eating their frugal meal which they bring with them in neat baskets, or romping across the lawns, the heart involuntarily exclaims, "God bless them!" and send unceasing work to their willing hands and those of their children and children's children that they may never be tempted to raise them for wrongdoing because of the lack of enforced idleness, or dire necessity. Some of these girls are orphans or lame, or deformed, or very miserable, and on the slender threads wound about their bobbins hangs their whole means of honest existence. The Brazza schools are conducted on the principle of a sweepstakes, each one being rewarded according to her deserts, and the work is paid for by the piece, the prices fluctuating according to the amount that can be realized by the sale of the lace produced, the standard for prices being taken from that of the wholesale Paris market, new and original designs commanding naturally a higher price than those more hackneyed. At the end of the year, prizes are distributed to the most regular, best and

cleverest workers of each separate school and a grand prize for
the first among all the schools; but like in a race among young
colts, the last sometimes carries off the honors, as she suddenly
blooms out into an artist of the bobbin, to the joy and surprise
of every one, and most of all of herself.   The schools of Brazza
exhibit the large album painted by Miss Celotte full of samples
of the girls ' laces and a quantity of their work mounted into objects for household use either by the girls themselves or by their
seamstress sisters, who are peasants also and trained for the purpose; pleading the excuse of a parent's loquacity, let us pass on to
the enumeration of the charitable institutions and industrial
schools, which also send exhibits.

INSTITUTION OF THE S. S. ECCE HOMO, NAPLES.

First among them ranks the Institution of the S. S. Ecce
Homo at Naples, not only for its size but because several of our
Lady Patronesses are on its Board of Direction.   This institution, which had lingered along as a sleepy refuge for indigent
old women and crippled children, sprang into glorious activity
during the terrible cholera scourge of 1885, which swept away all
the grown people of innumerable poor Neapolitan families and
left hundreds of miserable ragged orphans to wander starving
about the streets.   Daily the institution, Christ-like in action as
in name, gathered scores of these hungry little innocents under
its fondling care, and the King, the government, and the city
helped in the good work so that to-day it contains 350 inmates
and instructs 280 day scholars, many of whom belong to the most
wretched classes, who send their daughters to learn different
trades suited to impecunious women in its great industrial school-
rooms often tempted solely by the thought of the bodily strength-
ening to be obtained from its nourishing soups which are furnished at midday to all the scholars.   Here are made all kinds
of laces copied, the antique qualities of Valenciennes, Venetian
point, Cardiglia, Reticella, Torchon, Neapolitan, Abruzzi and
Milan point fugio, and added to this a wonderful new lace evolved
while copying the exquisite Gothic designs published by Padre
Pissicelli in the Paleographia of Monte Cassino, a book which is
exhibited in our small collection of designs for lace.

SIGNORA ENRICA FRASCHETTI.

Other beautiful reproductions of Cardiglia and Reticella equal to the rarest antique laces of this quality are exhibited by Signora Fraschetti, a most distinguished artist who has been honored by orders from Her Majesty the Queen, and is appreciated as the producer of the finest and most exquisite work in this style now made. Her address is Via della Carita 68, Rome.

THE SCHOOL OF SAN RANIERI, PISA.

An industrial school of which the Lady Patroness, Countess Agostini Venerosi della Seta, is one of the most active directresses is that of San Ranier at Pisa, which exhibits an album composed of samples of lace well executed. This school was instituted in the middle of the last century by the Grand Duke of Tuscany, to teach weaving as a means of instructing the girls of the poorest class among the townsfolk in the useful industry of weaving; but this trade, as well as that of straw plaiting, met with no success, and so the institution was gradually changed into an industrial school in the modern sense of the word, in which hand and machine knitting and sewing, the making of artificial flowers and of needle and bobbin lace, decorative designing and embroidery , cooking, washing and such rudiments of education as are adapted to women of humble extraction are taught. This metamorphosis into the existing type of an Italian industrial school was accomplished in 1879, and here, as in all these kind of institutions, there are always more applications for admittance than can be accepted, although about three hundred pupils are in constant attendance and the maximum time consecrated to the instruction of one pupil is three years.

THE SCHOOLS OF SAN PELEGRINO, BOLOGNA, AND SAN PAOLO, MODENA.

Schools established on the same system are those of the institution of San Pelegrino at Bologna, which exhibits two beautiful samples of its work in lace and Sicilian trapunto and the Educatorio di St. Paolo in Modena, from which Her Majesty, the Queen, who is patroness, sends an artistic and perfectly em-

broidered screen executed for her by the girls who enjoy the
immense advantage of having the artistic branch of their education under the supervision of Count Gandini and can embroider,
quickly and perfectly, copies of any of the celebrated antique
pieces of Italian work contained in the remarkable collection of
textiles at the museum, which has been made by him and bears
his name. This collection has already been copied by order of
Her Majesty for two German industrial schools, to the great advantage and instruction, not only of the girls of San Paolo, who
did the work, but of the hundreds of foreign children who were
thus enabled to profit by the inspiration of the unique possessions
of the Modenese museum in the development of their artistic
training.

THE ASYLUM OF THE FIGLIE DI MARIA.

On the western slopes of the mountainous island of
Sardignia, which rises like an immense foot out of the
Mediterranean, surrounded by its shoals of smiling islets,
is perched the picturesque city of Sassari, where, in 1832,
seven poor orphan girls were taken charge of by a benevolent soul and placed under the pine trees and among the olive
groves in a tiny private house, that they might no longer wander
about homeless and unkempt. This was the lowly foundation of
the great institution still called by the name given to these children, that of "Figlie di Maria" (daughters of Mary), which under
the direction of the Grey Sisters of Saint Vincent di Paolo, has
gradually grown and been transformed into the center from
which education, civilization and all the virtues emanate to the
moral advancement of the whole island; for under the wise administration of the able Suor Agostini Gassini, no less than
fifteen hundred orphans, deaf and dumb or abandoned children,
or little ones whose mothers are otherwise occupied, or rich
girls whose parents desire them to profit by the remarkable
educational advantages offered through the exceptional instruction provided by the cultured women, are daily taught and cared
for in the various departments of this great beehive, which in-
cludes also night-schools for men and women of the most

wretched classes, so that the tremendous influence for good of this far-reaching establishment can be imagined.

We can only speak here of the deaf and dumb children, who are the exhibitors of the net lace contained in the album marked with the name of this institution. Their intelligent, merry faces are reproduced in the photographs placed with their work, and no casual observer would believe they belonged to poor mutes. The reason is easily found, for the motherly hearts of these childless Grey Sisters have appreciated the longings of the maimed, for the companionship of the more blessed normal children; and so the mutes, daughters of Mary, during the meal and play hours, are thrown constantly with the sound orphans, and amid smiles and romps and gestures, they begin to imitate their young companions, and, guided during the hours of lessons by the trained wisdom of the sisters, quickly learn to lisp the few uncertain words which they possess the power of articulating. But even better than the physical is the moral effect of this system, the characters wound into sympathetic action by this busy common life, and no words can depict the transformation from sad moroseness to gay kindliness which occurs in the poor deaf mutes who bask in the sunshine of this sweet and simple, though great community.

ORPHANAGE OF ST. SILVESTRO, FLORENCE.

Another orphanage and refuge for abandoned children, that of St. Silvestro, Borgo Pinto 14, Florence, sends a large album and six photographs of laces, which have been executed by inmates of this establishment which is greatly assisted in its noble work through the proceeds obtained from the sale of its excellent lace by peddling it from house to house and in the hotels of Florence.

INSTITUTION OF ST. TERESA AND THE LEOPOLDINE SCHOOLS, FLORENCE.

Another album contains samples of the work executed in the institution of Santa Teresa, Via dei Serragli 108, which is one of the poorest schools in Florence, and is under the guidance of the Teresian nuns.

An album also contains the lace samples sent by another Florentine institution in which the young idea is taught to shoot and the young fingers are trained to useful occupations, called the Leopoldine Industrial School, which is conducted on the same principle as that of San Raineri at Pisa.

SCHOOL OF CANTU.

Two immense portfolios represent the species of work executed by the pupils of a different kind of industrial school—that in which only one kind of trade and the designing for it is taught. The samples they contain are from the school of art applied to the manufacture of lace, which exists in the small town of Cantu, situated near the picturesque Lake Como, and forming the center of one of the greatest lace producing regions of Italy. This industry was planted here in the sixteenth century by nuns of the Benedictine order who had a convent in the neighborhood, and until about fifty years ago was confined to the production of torchons and simple qualities of lace. To appreciate what it was at that period and the rapid progress since made, compare the work of the school exhibited in these portfolios or in those of the Cantuese producers with the album sent from Ascoli Piceno by the lady patroness from the Marche, Signora Tenti, which is composed of the most rudimentary quality of pillow lace, for to such depths has fallen the once celebrated lace industry of Offida, which is noticeable for its remarkable cheapness alone; or else compare it with the collection of simple samples of the laces worked in the Valley of Aosta sent by one of the lady patronesses from Piedmont, the Countess Francesetti. Both these ladies trust that, in obtaining a ready sale for their simple laces, the poor workwomen will be encouraged, and the antique industry can be revived, with its former elaborate perfection. Lace at Cantu is mostly produced as an accessory to the other occupations of the inhabitants. Many factories exist in this part of the country, and the fields here are rich and require much work at certain seasons; and so, whenever a spare moment is found amid the cares of housekeeping, the mother picks up her cushion and sets the bobbins flying, the children

come home from school, and, fetching their cushions, seat themselves beside her; and later, when the factories close and the sun
has set upon the fields, the grown-up daughters come home, and
taking the remaining cushions, set merrily to work, while
recounting the simple adventures and gossip of the day. This
kind of sociable, busy life can but produce an elevating effect
upon the morals of a community, and it has been noticed that
wherever ·this industry of lace-making flourishes, the people
deservedly enjoy the reputation of being both thrifty and moral.
About ten thousand women work at lace-making in the immediate neighborhood of Cantu alone, and a great many more support their families by this same means in other parts of the
province.

The work is produced either independently and sold to
merchants who go from house to house for the purpose of buy-
ing it, or is brought to the weekly market like butter or eggs; at
other times it is executed upon the designs and with the guidance
furnished by the shopkeepers and lace merchants of Cantu,
who, some of them, send representatives to travel from city to
city at certain seasons, selling the produce of their homes to
the great shops or have branch establishments in one city or
another. Many of the lace-makers, however, work entirely by
contract for the great lace emporiums and are not allowed to sell
to other purchasers any lace produced on the designs furnished
to them. Among others, the establishments of Jesurum, at
Venice and Paris, find it worth while to have certain work for
which the Cantuese enjoy a special reputation executed in this
way and I seize the opportunity to thank in the name of the Committee the Cavaliere Michangelo Jesurum, head of these houses, for
the flattering interest he has evinced in our undertaking and the
loan of some of the beautiful polichrome laces made at his
Venetian school of Maria Pia, to complete the illustration of the
present condition of Italian lace-making. The last named system is
defective, for the producer is very poorly paid, and the middle-
man is in constant fear of being crushed between the anvil and
hammer; but fortunately many of these Cantuese merchants
through inheritance or personal industry have obtained a small

private capital which enables them to stand alone to the advantage of their workwomen, of their own self-respect and of the public. The cleverest among these are the following who have produced really artistic work and have already been the recipients of distinctions, medals and diplomas at various exhibitions:

ANTONIA MERONI, CANTU.

Antonia Meroni, who is the head of an intelligent, kindly and clever family and most honorable in all her dealings, and therefore a favorite among the lady patronesses, sends with our exhibit an album containing samples of perfectly executed lace and a large collection entered for competition and sale, consisting of beautifully executed laces, the designs of which are taken from the antique, also Duchess silk, Blonde and torchon laces of superior quality. Large orders for pillow lace can be more quickly executed by the firms of Cantu and those of Liguria than in the schools, because they have more skilled hands at their command, but the object of our organization meets this difficulty by distributing the work when necessary among several different producers, so as to satisfy a great demand in the shortest possible space of time.

COLOMBO, CANTU.

Angelo, and Giuseppina Colombo, exhibit an album containing of 127 samples as well as a quantity of lace for sale, which is superior by far to the samples and contains pretty veils, scarfs and handkerchiefs in Duchess Blonde and antique lace.

MARELLI BENEDETTA, CANTU.

Marelli Benedetta and Vittorio Gabri, of Cantu, is the present head of a very old firm, and exhibits also an album of samples and a large quantity of torchon silk, Blonde and guipure lace, besides distinguishing herself by the production of fine black Brussels lace, scarfs and shawls, some of which is contained in our collection. She is well known because of the exactness of execution of all of her designs.

The family of Marelli also founded in 1821 through one of its daughters, Maria Marelli, who married an Arnaboldi and settled at

Carinate, near Cantu, founding the firm now belonging to Vittorio Gabri, which employs about 650 lace-makers and was established and flourished for many years owing to orders received from France. This house has always enjoyed an enviable reputation for the excellent quality of its pretty patterns and especially for the delightful softness of its silk blondes.

LIGURIA.

Another great and productive center of lace-making is the beautiful Riviera di Levante, between the ports of Genoa and Spezzia. Strangers who linger in the Alps Maritimes cannot imagine the charm of this exquisite region when the Riviera di Ponente has already become hot, dusty and enervating, and in consequence this favored region enjoys two seasons, that of the strangers in winter and of the Italians in summer, who find it more beneficial than watering places farther away from home, as it possesses the rare combination of sea and mountain air, with a good warm surf greatly charged with salt and iodine.

But the foreign visitors of the winter months and the compatriots who flock hither in the summer pause alike to watch the diligent lace-makers, who sit peacefully at home attending to their household duties and supporting themselves and their little ones by the yards and yards of snowy lace which roll off the cushion from under their flying fingers, while their husbands on fishing smacks and ships scour the sea to bring home a patrimony for the children.

Genoa is the center of the lace trade, but Sta Margarita and Rapallo are the two villages which produce the largest quantity of pillow lace, while Chiavari, on the same coast, is entirely devoted to that specialty of the Riviera the graceful knotted lace fringes for household linen called Macrame.

CHIAVARI.

Vincenzo Badarucco and Nicola Bianchi exhibit a quantity of artistic towels executed in this antique Moorish work.

RAPALLO.

The lace-makers of Rapallo who exhibit under the patronage of the wife of the mayor, Signora Castagnetta Ricci, have sent an album composed of leaves, each dedicated to a different exhibition.

The school or the Providenza comes first in this portafoglio, and followed by Nicoletta Castagnetta Tessara, whose beautifully executed laces have received diplomas and medals. Next come the samples from the long-established shops of Luigia Campodonico, who also exhibits laces of thread and silk and has enjoyed in the past both medals and diplomas for her products. Teresa Canevaro sends all the kinds of laces which are made in the neighborhood of Genoa, such as Point de Lille, Malines, Chantilly, etc.; like many of the others she has also enjoyed distinctions, but as we desire all these laces to stand or fall on their own merits, we will cease the lengthy enumeration of their qualifications.

Maria Schiattino and Quirolo exhibit samples and laces of the same type as the above, as also Gherardelli Campodonico.

Rosa Lanata also makes every variety of Ligurian lace, but her specialty is an artistic quality of Chantilly and she exhibits in it a pretty design of roses of which she sold a quantity to Her Majesty, the German Empress Frederik, on her last visit to the Riviera. Angelo Morelli and Gaetano Vassallo, Colombo Caprili and Anna Barbieri, all exhibit the same qualities of lace but without samples.

SANTA MARGHERITA.

The following are the exhibitors from the neighboring commune of Santa Margherita. The most celebrated is of course the firm of Angela Baffico, whose intelligent enterprise has been mentioned as the cause of the present prosperity of the lace trade in Liguria. Lorenzo Barbagelata sent an album as well as a quantity of lace principally by the yard, and a fine deep flounce of Chantilly made in one piece with hundreds of bobbins.

Felice Foppiano exhibits laces and Marianna Marigliano sends samples, but accompanied as are the goods of several other exhibitions by a pillow with lace upon it in process of fabrication.

Nana Raffo Costa makes a specialty of Blondes, point de Lille and Duchess laces.

SAMPIERDARENA.

From Sampierdarena almost within the gates of Genoa Ernestina Gavotti sends most artistic lace *fugio* and old Genoese point perfectly executed in gold and silver or in white thread. Her lace is of the highest merit and deserves to be universally copied in Liguria, as she has returned to the original type of work for which this part of Italy was celebrated. From the city of Genoa, Giuseppe Russo exhibits a large collection of samples of modern laces made in Liguria, and Doctor Vittorio Macchiavello, to pannels illustrative of the development of lace making in the same province.

PERUGIA.

The ladies of Perugia exhibit an album which contains 101 samples of modern lace which they manufacture in their leisure hours, but this is not the only modern lace sent to Chicago from Perugia; we have already mentioned the superb antique volume of Veccelio full of designs and samples which belonged to a suppressed religious order of that city, and the nuns since the secularization of their convents without losing any of their delicate taste for needle work have become a busy race and do not only direct the children in the asylums and nurse the sick in the hospitals, but they gather around them the miserable and disoccupied everywhere. Some of the gentle sisterhood have descended to the lowest steps of abnegation and in their humility have undertaken the superintendence and instruction of the most debased class of womankind, that of the female convicts in the prisons, in order that by their constant presence and loving, pitying care they may redeem them, if possible, and show that they are lost by association and not by nature. To these the teaching of lace has proved invaluable, not only interesting the artistic temperament of the women but permitting long hours of personal civilizing intercourse, unsuspected by the shy outcasts who learn at the same time a trade which furnishes them with an easy means of support for the first moments of sad

liberty, the want and misery of which often inspire to fresh deeds
of crime.   The album composed of beautifully executed samples
of torchon and Brussels pillow lace is exhibited by the sisters of
Providence and worked under their direction in the great
woman's prison at Perugia, and a smaller album comes from another female prison at Messina where pillow laces and Sicilian
drawn work are perfectly copied from the antique.

TUSCAN HOMESPUNS.

Another field of the sisters' activity in Tuscany is illustrated
by the rich-toned material which covers the walls and drapes the
windows of the Italian section, and they send a sample composed
of varied specimens of this quality of picturesque homespun
made upon hand looms by the peasant girls of Tuscany under
the direction of Suor Denis and the Sisters of Charity at Miglio-
rano, province of Pisa, where these indefatigable women, with
no capital but faith and perseverance, have struggled on and
planted a flourishing, artistic and worthy, though modest industry, the material which they use being of the best, and the combination of effect chosen with the unerring good taste, which is
peculiarly the attribute of high ladies of culture, no matter what
humble garb may conceal their identity. These noble women hope
that the appreciation of their artistic products, which must arise
when they are known, will bring them many orders which would
enable them to increase the looms, employing a larger number of
destitute girls and forming a small capital.   The fringe is also
woman's work, being dyed and woven by Maddalena Salvadori
Calle di Pietro, No. 5087 San Bartolomeo, Venice, whose specialty is the copying of antique fringes.   In cotton bought at
wholesale prices, which would procure for them the possibility
of selling more cheaply the artistic materials, dress cottons and
coarse homespuns, which are purely woman's work and essentially original as being produced without any assistance whatever
from the stronger sex.

But the gentle nuns have occupations further afield wherever
there is ignorance and misery, and they do not hesitate in their
self-abnegation to seek the most distant lands in which to culti-

vate the industrious possibilities dormant in the laziest savage nature. They only imitate the example set by their sisters of the sixteenth century, who meekly followed on the destructive pathway of the fierce and brutal conquerors of Peru and Mexico, striving to bind up some of the hearts which they had broken and cure a few of the wounds inflicted by their barbarity. They sought too with the healing balm of Christian charity to soothe the distraught minds of the poor aborigines committed to their charge and to train the trembling hands to firm self-reliance through the practical arts of industrious peace.

They caused the men to build houses and churches under their supervision, while they taught the women to sew and make lace to adorn the altars of Him for love of whom they had donned their rough garb and toiled so patiently among the desolate races, and their work was not in vain, as is proved by the curious lace numbered 599, which has become identified with the inhabitants of Paraguay, and by the lace-makers still found among the Pacific coast Indians of North America, who have been considered worthy to form part of the great World's Fair, which constitutes the apotheosis of woman's development throughout the ages.

The Italian Missionary Nuns of to-day follow in the footsteps of their predecessors, humbly thanking God that the inventions of the nineteenth century render their tasks less arduous, and in Ceylon and the islands of the archipelago, in far Japan and isolated China (See Nos. 619 and 697 cases) in every land where the Catholic Church has penetrated, they train the girls in womanly occupations so that the little heathen orphans intrusted to their instruction owe to them among many other useful occupations a knowledge of lace-making, which if made use of with industry, even should other means fail, would always keep them from misery and starvation.

Since history began, Italy has ever marched in the vanguard of progress, and when in the centuries that followed the fall of the Roman Empire under the repeated barbarian invasions, all Europe was one battle-field of strife and bloodshed engendered by ignorance, hatred, malice and all uncharitableness, fair Italy

awoke first to her shame, and raising her head, shook off the insidi-
ous barbarism of the middle ages, which was trying to destroy all
record of her great Latin past, and uprose with a mighty determination to redeem her reputation, and recivilize and educate
mankind.   The other nations of Europe stood awestruck by the
products of her fertile genius.   The writings of her great sons
penetrated to the uttermost of the continent and quickened the
hearts and souls of intelligent men to higher aspirations.   The
beautiful remnants of her frail laces, stranded in every town of
civilization, are but the straws left by the current to indicate
where its vivifying waters have passed.   But, alas, the taste of
these was very sweet and strong and proved as intoxicating as
the wines from the Sicilian vineyards, and each nation determined to call the fountain head its own, so that the clamor of
strife again re-echoed from the Alps to the Apennines and once
more the sons of the soil were ground down beneath an usurping
foreign heel.

The powers of to-day still gaze longingly toward the sunny
hills and blue skies of United Italy, and the young nation is
forced to spend all that she can earn to arm herself to the teeth
and defend her hearth and home against the covetous, instead
of using it upon the education of her poorest children.

O proud and rich Columbia, if you want the Italians to
remain at home and keep far from your cities and your ports,
open these instead to their trade.   Let the oil and the fruits and
the silk and the flax, the beautiful artistic carvings in wood and
stone, the original paintings and the reproduction of the glorious works of the past, the soft laces and the rich embroideries
executed by the women, enter your land in their stead.

The Italians love their simple homes with a passion that is
unquenchable and will bless you for the alternative.   Oh cause
your happy citizens to think on the pleasant weeks of travel they
have enjoyed among the beautiful views of Italy, the foreground
ever composed of wondrous monuments and works of art, cause
them to think of the potent charm which has moved them in
your theaters as in their own houses, while listening to the
superb music of Italian composers, the rich voices of Italian

singers: or when alone beside their hearths the winters' cold, the summer heat have been alike forgotten in conning the enchanting description of Virgil, Pliny, Tasso, Petrarch, Manzoni and half a hundred others, cause them to think on the teachings of St. Augustine of Savanarola and of Galileo to which they and the world owe so much, and on the emotion they experienced when first stirred by the overwhelming, awful language of great Dante—and the next time they have to do with poor benighted Italian emigrants, let them remember that the same rich soil gave birth to poet and peasant alike.

And if this fails to touch their hearts and still the charitable American's desire to close your doors on these brothers in faith and feature, whose only fault is a neglected education, let them pause and remember, God did not send one of the great Italians in 1492 across the ocean to discover an " America for the Americans;" these existed already in your first dusky sons, who have been cruelly sacrificed to the exigencies of progress, but to found a home full of prosperity and freedom, alike for the persecuted and the enterprising sons of all Europe, in which they might create a strong new nation. Cristofero Colombo of Genoa, who sailed from Spain with a crew composed of the most reckless souls from all the ports of the Mediterranean coast, brought no money in his hand, no treasures in his ships; his riches were *intelligence* and *will;* the early settlers, fleeing from persecution, were no better provided, and as the centuries have rolled on and you have grown rich and powerful, the personal condition and the character of the Italians who seek your shores has not changed.

Oh, hearken, fair mighty, glorious Columbia, God-child and namesake of the great Genoese, it is one of your own daughters who calls to you across the waters he traversed in search of you; close not your doors against his kinsmen last in the throng you shut out one of his own children, heir to his genius to which you owe your **very** being.   CASTELLO DI BRAZZA.

MARCH 11, 1893.

PART VI.

List of the names of the ladies forming the subscribers and Committee for the Italian Lace Exhibit in the Woman's Building at the World's Columbian Exhibition in Chicago, United States, America, during the summer of 1893.

Initiaters constituted into a Board of Administration.

The Countess Cora A. di Brazza Savorgnan nata Slocomb, elected president and representative of the Committee in America.

Her Excellency the Marchioness Paula Res di Villamarina, Grand mistress of ceremonies to Her Majesty the Queen.

The Countess Teresa Agostini Venerosi della Seta (replacing her mother, Countess Andriana Marcello, deceased). Lady in waiting to Her Majesty.

Princess Elizabeth Brancaccio di Trigiano nata Field, Lady of the palace to Her Majesty.

Countess Maria Pasolini nata Ponti.

General Secretary and Italian Correspondent, Signorina Dorina Bearzi : assistant, Signorina Victoria Fanna.

Address CLAVIANO, Provincia di Udine.

Secretary in America,

SIGNORA EVA MARIOTTI.

Italian Section Woman's Building, Chicago.

I. ANCIENT VENETIA.

DIVIDED INTO TWO PARTS—VENETIA AND FRIULI.

1st. Venetia—Capital Venice.

	Lire.
Directress.—Countess Andriana Marcello (deceased) for the lady in waiting to Her Majesty—School of Burano................ .	800
Patronesses.—Duchess Biancha Bianci di Casalanza, Mogliano......	100
Signora Teresa Paccagnello, nata Pigazzi, Mogliano............	100
Countess Maria Bonin, nata Nievo, Vicenza....................	100
Countess Carolina Colleoni, nata Ginstiniani Bandini, Vicenza....	100
Princess Giovanelli, nata Chigi....	
Lady of the Palace to Her Majesty Lonigo.....................	100
Countess Loredana di Porto nata Bonin, Vicenza.............	100
Countess della Torre, Vicenza	100
Countess Maria degli Azzoni Avagadro, Padua................	103
Signora Stefania Embone, Padua	100
Countess Papafava dei Carraresi, nata Menicone Bracceschi, Padua.........................	100
Signora Anaïs Forlani, Padua	100
Countess Brandolin, nata d'Adda, Lady of the Palace to Her Majesty, Venice........................·......	100
Mrs. Arthur Bronson, Venice...........................	100
Mrs. Robert Browning, Venice	100
Countess Eleanor Papadopoli, nata Hellenbach, Lady of the Palace to Her Majesty, Venice	100
Countess Miniscalchi Errizo, nata Ponti, Verona...............	100
Total Venetia...	2403

2d. Friuli—Capital Udine.

	Lire.
Directress of Province.—Countess Cora di Brazza Savorgnan, nata Slocomb—for Lace School of Brazza........................	800
Collected......................................	285
Patronesses—Mrs. G. Pendleton Bowler................	100
Mrs. Cuthbert Slocomb	100
Signorina Jenny Cecconi ⎱ of Mount Ceccon .... Signorina Elvira Cecconi ⎰	200
Directress, City of Udine.—Contessina Vittoria Cecconi Beltrame....	210
Signora Camilla Pecile...........................	160
Signora Elio Morpurgo	150
Countess Veradi Brazza, Marchesa Simonetti..................	100

Contessina Giulia di Concina 100
Signora Emilia Girardelli Muratti of Trieste 100

Total Friuli 2305

N. B.—II. Total Venetia................ ....Lire, 4708

II. ROMAN PROVINCES.

LIRES.

Directresses.—Her Excellency Marchesa Paula Pes di Villamarina.
  1. The Grand Mistress of Ceremonies to Her Majesty, Rome... 100
  2. Princess Elizabetta Brancaccio di Trigiano, nata Field, Rome. 400
Italian Patronesses.—Signora Antoinette Costa.................... 120
  Countess Barbiellini Amidei, nata Lewis Rome................. 100
  Countess Caprara, Rome.................................... 100
  Marchesa Gravina, Rome................................... 100
  Countess Giannotti, nata Kinney, Rome..................... 100
  Countess Santa Fiora, nata Santa Croce....................
  Lady of the Palace to Her Majesty, Rome................... 100
  Marchesa di San Severino, Rome........................... 100
  Countess Ada Telfner, nata Hungerford, Rome.............. 100
  Marchesa Vanni, Pasqua, Rome............................ 100
  Princess di Venosa, Lady of the Palace to Her Majesty, Rome... 100
  Duchess Lante, nata Davis, Viterbo........................ 100

Total.. 1,420
Foreign Patronesses residing in Rome:—Mrs. Orville Horwitz, of
  Baltimore 300
  Mrs. Stanley Hazeltine, of Philadelphia..................... 100
  Mrs. Hungerford, of California............................ 100
  Mrs. Nathan Sargent, American Legation................... 100

Foreign patronesses, total............................ 600
Italian Patronesses................................... 1,420

II. Total, Roman provinces........................ 2,020

III. TUSCANY.

LIRES.

Directress of Province.—Countess Teresa Agostini Venerosa della
  Seta, nata Marcello—Pisa............................... 420
Patronesses.—Countess Larderel, Leghorn.................... 120
  Signora Maria Mimbelli, Leghorn......................... 100

The ancient divisions of Italy are ranked in this list according to the sums of money collected within the provinces which compose them.

Other ladies of Leghorn	110
Countess Bernardi, Lucca	180
Signora Costanza Huffer, Lucca	100
Other ladies of Lucca	40
Total	1,076

2. Capital Florence.

	LIRES.
Directress.—Marchesa Anna Torregiani, nata Fry	210
Patronesses.—Princess Anna Cortsini, nata Barberini, Lady of the Palace to Her Majesty	100
Marchesa Gentile Farinola, Lady of the Palace to Her Majesty	100
Mrs. Fahestock, of New York	100
Countess Josephine della Gherardesca, nata Fischer	100
Marchesa di Montagliari	100
Marchesa Lily Spinola, nata Page	100
Marchesa Giulia Torregiani, Lady of the Palace to Her Majesty	100
Total, Florence	910
2. Other cities	1,079
III. Total, Tuscany	1,989

IV. SICILY.

	Lire.
Directress for Messina, Countess Marullo—Lady of the Palace to Her Majesty and a Committee of Ladies organized by her in Messina	958
Directress for Palermo. Unelected Patronesses—Princess Sofia Trabia di Butero, nata Galeotto—Lady of the Palace to Her Majesty.	225
Princess Baucina—Lady of the Palace to Her Majesty	100
Princess Sofia Belmonte Montroy—Lady of the Palace to Her Majesty	100
Signora Tomaso Crudeli	100
Signora Florio	100
Countess Mazzarino—Lady of the Palace to Her Majesty	100
Princess Maria di Sant Elia nata Menebua—Lady in Waiting to Her Majesty	100
Signora Tina Whitaker	100
Palermo total	925
Total Messina	958
IV. Total Sicily	1883

V. LOMBARDY.

	Lire.
Directress. Marchesa Maria Trotti—Lady in Waiting to Her Majesty	150
Patronesses for Milan. Signora Cramer, nata Pourtales	160
Marchesa Maura di Cassini, Nata Ponti	100
Marchesa Isimbardi	100
Signora Remingia Ponti	100
Signora Virginia Ponti	100
Countess Erminia Sala nata Trotti—Lady of the Palace to Her Majesty	100
Princess Ida Visconti di Modroni	100
1. Total Milan	910

Patronesses for Other Cities.

Countess Suardi nata Ponti, Bergamo	200
The Administrative Committee of the Industrial School at Cantu	100
Signora Ester Isingrini, nata Ponti Monza	100
Countess Gwendolina della Somaglia, nata Doria—Lady of the Palace to Her Majesty, Monza	100
Signora Charles Leonino, Varese	100
2. Other cities	600
Total Milan	910
V. Total Lombardy	1510

VII. ROMAGNA.

	Lire.
Directress—Countess Maria Pasolini, nata Ponti for the school of Cocolia, by Ravenna	800
Collected	120 00
Patronesses—Marchesa Virginia di Mazzocorato Bologna	167 50
Duchess Massari-Ferrara	100 00
VI. Total—Romagna	1,187 50

VII. LIGURIA.

	Lire.
Directress—Marchesa Fiammetta Doria—Lady of the Palace patronesses to Her Majesty, Genoa	700
Princess Camilla Centurione Scotti, Genoa	100
Total—Genoa	800

Other Cities.

Duchess Canevero di Zoagi, Chiavari	200
Signora Castagnetto Ricci, Rapallo	100
Total—other cities	300
Total—Genoa	800
VII. Total—Liguria	1,100

VIII. NAPLES.

	Lire.
Directress—Donna Maria Spinelli dei principe di Scalia	100
Patronesses—Baroness Baracco, Lady of the Palace to Her Majesty.	100
Princess Colonna Stigliano, nata Mackay	100
Signora Sofia di Luca, nata Kennedy	100
Princess di Moliterno, Lady of the Palace to Her Majesty	100
Princess Pignatelli Strongoli, Lady in waiting to Her Majesty	100
Marchesa Santasilia	100
Duchess Tommacelle della Torre nata Haight	100
Baroness Tosti	100
VIII. Total, Naples	900

IX. PIEDMONT.

	Lire.
Patronesses—The Ladies of Her Majesty	150
Baroness Blanc	100
Countess Natalie Francesetti nata della Rocca	100
Countess Incisa di San Stefano nata Sambaz	100
IX. Total, Piedmont	450

X. EMILIA.

Patronesses—Marchesa Rita Schedoni, nata Princess Manoukbey, Modena	135
Conntess Gaddi, nata Pepoli, Lady of the Palace to Her Majesty, Forlim popoli	125
Total, Emilia	260

XI. UMBRIA.

Patronesses—Marchesa Chigi Zondadare, Sienna	100
Countess Memieore Braceeschi nata Brazza-Savorgnan, Perugia	100
XI. Total, Umbria	200

XII. ABRUZZI.

Patroness—Marchesa Cappelli, nata Hirsch, Aquila......Total...... 100

XIII. MARCHE.

Patroness—Signora Antoinetta Tinti Ascoli-Picena.......Total..... 100

XIV. SARDEGNA.

Signorina Giordano Apostoli Sassari.................... Total..... 100

BOOKS COLLECTED BY ORDER OF MR. CHRISTOPHER R. CUMMINGS, OF CHICAGO.

677. L'Ecole de Dentelles a Burano Venezia Imprimierie. Kirchmayr & Scotti, 182-.

678. I Merletti ad Ago o a Punto in Aria di Burano. Richiamo Storico di Pasqualigo Co., Dr. Giuseppe, Treste, Tipografia, Pastori, 1887.

679. Cenni sull' Industria dei Merletti. Michel Angelo, Jesurum, Venezia, Tipografia del Commercio.

680. La Stor.a della Conquista di Due Medaglie d'Oro. Merletti di Venezia, nel 1878, da Fambri, Firenze, Tipografia, Lemonnier, 1879.

681. I Merletti nel Circondario di Chiavari. G. B. Brignardello, Firenze, Tipografia G. Barbeca, 1873.

682. Scavi di Claterna nel Comune di Ozzano dell' Emilia. Roma, Tipografia della R. Accademia dei Lincei, 1892.

683. Designs for Point Lace. W. Barnard, 119 Edgeware Road, London.

684. Hand-book of Point Lace. W. Barnard, 119 Edgeware Road, London.

685. La Paleografia Artistica nei Codici Cassinesi. Applicata a Lavori Industriali Merletti, dalla Tav. 1, alla Tav. 20, Litografia, Monte Cassino, 1888.

686. Descrizione di **Alcuni** Minutissimi Intagli a Mano. Properzia di Rossi.

687. Spitzen Munsterbuch Museum fur Kunst und Industrie. Wilhelm Hoffmans.

688. Histoire du Point **d'Alencon depuis son** origine jusqua **nos jours.** Mme. G. Despieures.

689. La Vita dei Veneziani nel, 1300. Le Vesti, B. Cecchetti.

690. Tessuti e Merletti Esposizione, 1887. Erculei.

691. Rapport sur les Dentelles, les Blondes, les Tulles par Felix Aubry. Esposition de Loudres.

692. Il Fiore delle Donne Italiane dall' Av. to Franciosi.

693. Lecons Pratiques pour Executer la Dentelle aux fuseaux, de la Bonne Managere.

694. Donne Illustri Italiane, Proposte ad Esempio, dedicata a S. M. la Regina Margherita per Eugenio Comba.

695. Histoire de la Dentelle par Mme. de X—., Paris, 1843.

696. Note per le Giovanette Studiose.

697. Alcune Donne Illustri Italiane di Giuseppe Spallicci.

698. La Dogaressa di Venezia per Pompeo Molmenti.

699. Costumi del Tre Cento.

700. Guide to Old and New Lace in Italy by the Countess Cora di Brazzä.

COLLECTION D'OUVRAGES ANCIENS SUR LA DENTELLE DE VENISE. FERD. ONGANIA, EDIT.

701. **Vecellio.**—Recueil des nobles et vertueuses dames, en quatre livres dans lesquelles on voit en 119 dessins toutes les especes de parements, de points ouvrages d'ornements, de fleurons, etc.; fac-simile de l' edition originale de 1600, etc. Venise, 1876 ....80 fr.

702. **Franco J.**—Nouvelle invention de divers ornements tels que le point en l' air, 24 dessins de dentelles, etc.; fac-simile de l' edition originale de 1596. Venise, 1877...................................20 fr.

703. **Lucrece Romaine.**—Ornements nobles pour toutes les elegantes dames, ouvrage contenant des cols, dentelles d'une tres grande beaute, 20 planches in-4°; fac-simile de l' edition originale de 1620. Venise, 1876, ... 30 fr.

704. **Pagan Math.**—Le bon exemple du desir louable qu' ont les dames d'une grande adresse a preparer les points ouvrages en feuillage, 31 planches gravees; fac-simile de l' edition originale de 1550. Venise, 1878..30 fr.

705. **Zoppino** (Nicolas d'Aristotile dit).—Recueil de belles broderies anciennes et modernes dans lequel une rare adresse soit d'homme soit de femme pourra s' exercer dignement avec l' aiguille, etc.; 52 planches gravees; fac-simile de l' edition originale de 1537. Venise, 1877...........30 fr.

706. **Vavassore And.** (dit Guadagnini).—Œuvre nouvelle universelle intitulee: Recueil de broderies ou les respectables dames et jeunes filles trouveront des ouvrages varies pour faire les cols de leurs camisoles, etc.; fac-simile de l' edition originale de 1546. Venise, 1878...........30 fr.

707. **Ostaus Jean.**—Tres belle maniere de tenir ses jeunes filles occupees, comme le faisait la chaste Lucrece Romaine avec ses femmes, alors qu' elle fut surprise, travaillant avec elles, par Tarquin accompagne de son mari; fac-simile de l' edition originale de 1567. Venise, 1878..30 fr.

708. **Pagan Mat.**—Ouvrage nouveau, redige par Dominique da Seva, dit le Franciosino, ou l'on enseigne a toutes les gracieuses demoiselles a travailler en toute sorte de points, etc.; fac-simile de l' edition originale de 1546. Venise, 1878...40 fr.

709. **Paganino Alex. (Burato)**—Livre premier des broderies au moyen duquel on apprend de differentes façons la maniere de broder, chose qui n' a encore jamais ete faite ni montree, maniere que le lecteur apprend en tournant la page; fac-simile de l' edition originale de 1527. Venise. 1878 ....40 fr.

710. **Serena.**—Nouvel ouvrage de broderies dans lequel ou trouve diverses sortes de points en natte et de points a fil, etc. Venise, Dominique de Franceschi; fac-simile de l' edition originale de 1594. Venise 1878, ... 30 fr.

711. **Zoppino (Aristotile dit).**—Exemplaire d' ouvrages ou les jeunes filles et les grandes dames pourront facilement apprendre la maniere de travailler, etc.; fac-simile de l' edition originale de 1530. Venise, 1878 . . . . .30 fr.

712. **Parasole Isabella Catanea.**—Joyau precieux des femmes vertueuses. Ou l' on voit de tres beaux travaux en point en l' air, a reseaux a maille et a fuseaux, dessines .par I. C. Parasole Publies de nouveau par Luchino Gargano; fac-simile de l' edition originale 1600. Venise, 1878. . . . . 40 fr.

713. **Tagliente.**—Nouvel exemplaire qui enseigne a coudrè et a broder aux femmes, et a dessiner a quiconque, etc., 1531.; fac-simile. Venise, 1879 . . . . .50 fr.

714. **Burato.**—Livre premier des broderies, au moyen duquel on apprend, etc. (voir N. IX. Paganino.)
   A. b. c.—Livre deuxieme, troisieme et quatrieme des broderies au moyen duquel on apprend la maniere de broder, etc. Ouvrage nouveau. Alex. Paganino 1527; fac-simile. Venise, 1880 (tres rare)...90 fr.

715. **Urbani de Gheltof G. M.**—Traite historique et technique de la frabication des dentelles venitiennes (Venise-Burano). In-12 avec 7 planches et 27 vignettes. Venise, 1878. . . . . .15 fr.
   La traduction en français par M. Le Monnier, *gratis.*

716. **Urbani de Gheltof G. M.**—A technical history of the manufacture of Venetian laces (Venice-Burano) in 12 with 7 engravings in fac-simile and 27 vignettes, translated by Lady Layard. Venise, 1888......15 fr.

VIENT DE PARAITRE: I. bis VECELLIO C.

717. **Corona Delle Nobili et Virtvuose Donne Libro Qvinto.**—Nel quale fi contengono molti, and varii Diffegni di diuerfe forti, and specialmente che feruono per Bauari ch'in Venetia fi coftumano, and in molte altre parti del mondo. Opera molto vtile, and neceffaria per quelle virtuofiffime Donne che fi dilettano di lauorare con Aco, punti in Aria, punti Tagliati, and a Reticelli, cosi fopra Cambradi, e Renfi, come fopra altre Tele. Venezia, appresso Cesare Vecellio, 1596. . Prix fr. 20

PARASOLE C.

718. **Teatro Delle Nobili et Virtvose Donne.**—Dove si rappresentano Varij Dissegni di Lauori nouamente Inuentati, et disegnati da Elisabetta Catanea Parafole Romana. Roma, 1616. . . . . Prix fr. 40

719. **Urbano di Gheltof Francese.**

720. **Corona delle Virtuose Donne.** Libro quinto, Vecellio, Venezia, 1590.

721. **Prima Parte de'Fiori e Disegno di Varie Sorti di Ricance Moderni come Merle, Bavari, Manichetti etc. in Venezia.** Appresso Francesco dei Franceschi, Senese all' Insegna della Pace.

722. **Catalogue Ongania.**

723. J. Beal, dentelles et broderies 145 planches.
724. J. Beal. Nouvelle edition dentelles anciennes, Paris chez Calaves 68. Que de Lafayette. Foglie 26.
725. **E. Kumsch.** Spitzen und Weiss Stickerei des XVI, XVIII, Jahrn. K. Kunst gewerbe Museum zu Dresden. Foglie 50.
726. Prof. B. Hoffman, director der K. Industrieschule Stilisirte Planzenformen in Industriella Verwendung. Serie I. Spitzen 12, blatt.
727. Photographs of Cluny Museum, published **by** A. Calavvas, **68 Rue** Lafayette, Paris, 35 foglie.
728. R. Forrer. Die Graeber und Textilunde von Achmin, **Panapolis.** Strassburg, 1891. Druck von Emil Birkhauser Basel.
729. R. Forrer. Romische und Byzantinische Seiden Textile aus den **Gaeber Felde von** Achmin Panopolis, Strassburg, i-e, 1891. Druck Emil Birkhauser Basel.
730. **Prehistorische Varia aus dem Unterhaltungsblatt fur Freunde** der **Alterthums kunde Antiqua.** Herausgegeben von R. Forrer und H. Messikommer Zurich, 1889.
731. **Reproduction of Ancient Lace Plates of the end of the last century, very rare, called:** Nova Espositore di Recami e Disegni alla Molto Illustre Signora Ippolita Manfredi appresso Giacomo Antonio Somascho.
732. **Quental Ornament und Stickmunsterbuch von Peter Quental, 1527–1529.** 80 Tafelm, Leipzig von A. M. Golze.
733. **Joh Sibmacher's Neues stick, Spitzen Musterbuch von Jahre, 1604.** Herausgegeben von Dr. Georgeus, Berlin, Ernest Wasmuth. 60 Tafeln, 2 boeder blatter.
734. **Livre d'Heures, editeur Alfred Mame et Fils, Tours, Dessins, Henri Carot, Illustre d'apres les Dentelles de toutes les Epoques et toutes les styles.** Foglie 300, e Introduction au sujet de la Dentelle.
735. **Guarich's Reprints of Rare Books.** III—Pagan Mathio, La Gloria et l'Honore de Punto Tagliato e Punto in Aere. Venezia, Mathio Pagan, 1558. London Bernard Guarlich 15. Piccadilly, 1884.
736. **Idem.**
737. **Parasole Isabella, Catania.**—Studio delle Virtuose Donne, Rome, Antonio Facchetti, 1597.
738. **Teresa Guattrocolo Giaglio, Guida ai Lavori Donneschi.** Libreria G. B. Petrini, Torino 15. Via Garibaldi, 1890.
739. **Alfredo Melani.**—Svaghi Artistici Femminili, Editore N. Hoepli, 1892.
740. **Livre de Dentelles No. 1.** Chez Amand Durand sous la Direction de Emmanuel Bocher. 69 Rue du Cardinal Lemoine, 1883. Foglie 20.
741. **Idem, No. 2.** Foglie, 20.
742. **Idem, No. 3.** Foglie, 10.
743. **Idem, No. 4.** Foglie, 21.
744. **Idem, No. 5.** Foglie, 20.

◁ INDEX. ▷

PART II.

The Birth of the Textile Arts and the Origin of Lace.

PART III.

The Renaissance.

PART V.

The Modern Lace. Its Artificers and Framing.

PART VI.

(near) "Nanduty" Lace - Sarapua Eo-

North west corner of Agricultural

Bldg- See Hamler. piece in Italy (?)
                        Coll - Value $20

Lace work. Mrs J. A. Brant
           DuBuque Iowa
           Elizabeth Anthony
            Clifton Iowa

1 to 89. inc 34 + 35 is
               duplicate
total: 89
        2
      ———
      91

Contessa Brazza

Life Italian peasant
women in country
$\&^2$ in City.

26ᵘ Sept
7 October
?

11 am at Assembly
Room Womens
building

LIBRO. DI LAVORIERI.

Alla Serenissima Sig.^{ra} MARGARITA GONZAGA da ESTE

DVCHESSA DI FERRARA,
Patrona Colendissima.

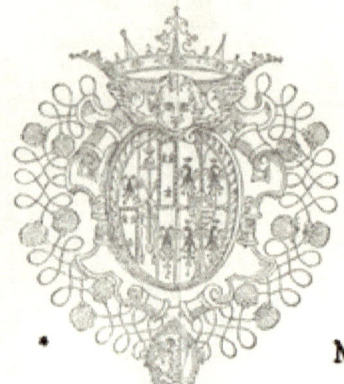

IN BOLOGNA.
Appresso Fausto Bonardi.
Con licenza de' Superiori.

M. D. XCI.

SERENISSIMA SIGNORA.

 Avendo io racolti questi varij diſſegni di lauori da me fatti in più volte, parte per compiacere ad alcuna di queſte Signore Bologneſi, & parte per proprio trattenimento in quell'hore che mi auanzano dalle occupationi mie ordinarie. Et eſſendomi riſſoluto di darli in luce à ſodisfattione delle virtuoſe Donne, coſi perſuaſo da alcuni amici, Non mi è ſtato di meſtiere l'andare molto penſando del nome di quale di eſſe particolarmente doueſſi ornarli la fronte, acciò più lietamente foſſe dall'vniuerſale di tutte riceuuto, peruche in vn ſolo girar d'occhi mi ſi è preſentata inanzi l'Altezza V. Ser.ma nù tàto per la eminenza del loco doue ella ſiede in Italia, quanto per la inclinatione che tiene à tutte le nobili arti, che à gràn Donna ſi còuengono, & à queſta in particolare: Onde auiene che coteſta Corte la quale à tutte l'altre d'Italia è ſtata ſempre eſſempio di coſtumi, & di virtù, hora più che mai fioriſca, & riſplèda ſotto i benigniſſimi inſtuſſi, & chiari raggi di lei, non eſſendoci hormai dubbio, che hoggi in Ferrara, ſi come nell'altre nobili arti, coſi in queſta ſi ſono tanto auanzate le induſtrioſe mani delle virtuoſe Donne, che poſſono i lauori, che da quelle eſcono, pareggiarſi non ſolo, ma anco giuſtamète anteporſi à quelli, che di Spagna, & Fiàdra portano tanto grido per tutto il Mondo. Queſte coſe mi hano perſuaſo facilmète, che ella lia per riceuere coſi picciol dono con la ſolita ſua benignità (al che fare humilſ.e la ſupplico,) & tanto più quanto ſpero che meno le habbia da eſſere di briga in diffenderlo da gli altrui morſi, non perche lo ſtimi ſenza imperfettione. mà per nò douete egli eſſer ſottopoſto ragioneuolmente alla cenſura di ſeuere perſone, anzi ſolamente di virtuoſe, & gentiliſſime Donne, che con ſincerità lo giudicheranno. Viua la Ser.ma Altezza V. felicisſima per molti Anni, che io in tanto humiliſſimamente con ogni riuerenza le bacio le mani. Di Bologna il dì 17. Agoſto. 1591.

Di V. A. Sereniſsima.

Humilis. & deuotiſſ. Seruitore.

A. P.